BOMB ISLAND

B⬛MB ISLAND

A NOVEL

STEPHEN HUNDLEY

HUB CITY PRESS
SPARTANBURG, SC

Cover Design: Meg Reid
Cover illustration: Kimber Fowler
Map illustration: Bailey Pillow
Interior Book design: Kate McMullen
Proofreaders: Corinne Segal / Iza Wojciechowska

Library of Congress
Cataloging-in-Publication

Names: Hundley, Stephen, 1991- author.
Title: Bomb Island : a novel Stephen Hundley.
Description: Spartanburg, SC : Hub City Press, 2024.
Identifiers: LCCN 2023045206 (print)
LCCN 2023045207 (ebook)
ISBN 9798885740258 (hardback)
ISBN 9798885740326 (epub)
Subjects: LCGFT: Bildungsromans. | Romance fiction. | Thrillers (Fiction). Novels.
Classification: LCC PS3608.U543 B66 2024 (print) | LCC PS3608.U543 (ebook) | DDC 813/.6--dc23/eng/20231204
LC record available at https://lccn.loc.gov/2023045206
LC ebook record available at https://lccn.loc.gov/2023045207

Hub City Press gratefully acknowledges support from the Chapman Cultural Center, National Endowment for the Arts, the Amazon Literary Partnership, and the South Carolina Arts Commission.

Manufactured in the United States
First Edition

HUB CITY PRESS
200 Ezell Street
Spartanburg, SC 29306
1.864.577.9349

To my grandparents.

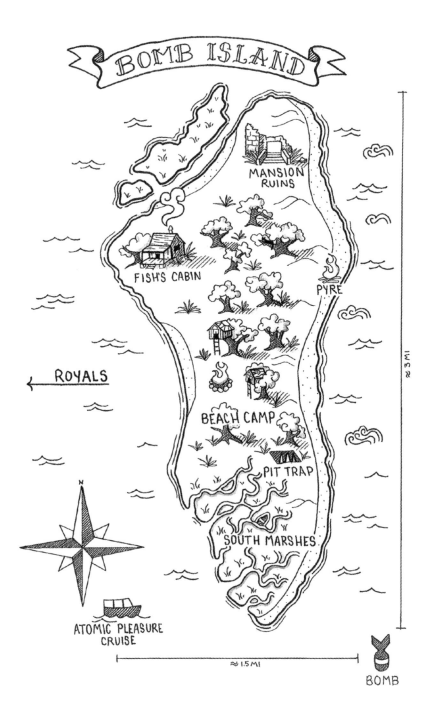

PART ONE

ONE

O n Bomb Island, the boy, Fish, lay on an oak branch and looked through a small pair of binoculars. A knot in the wood dug into his stomach and a mosquito whined near his ear, but he didn't move. He lived here with his family: the young man, Reef; the old man, Nutzo; and Whistle, their mother-sage. Ahead of him, on the windy gray beach, a white tiger stalked a skinny foal.

The tiger is my brother, Fish thought. I shouldn't be afraid. Whistle had told him so.

Where some of Georgia's barrier islands were little more than long-term sandbars, Bomb Island stretched three miles end-to-end and was a mile and a half across at its widest point. The oaks of the island were famous in the mainland town of Royals, where it was a point of pride that the ancient trees had been used to build

1

Washington's ships during the Revolution. The legend was that none of the Bomb Island ships had been sunk. More famous was the atomic bomb that had fallen, by accident, in 1955 and lodged in the seafloor.

The foal that the tiger was stalking stood at the base of a dune and turned its head to look each way down the beach. Its brown, fuzzy ears battled the stiff wind coming from the ocean. Sand, spray, and foam were carried in the air. The tiger moved in the shallow depressions between the dunes, creeping on its belly and hiding in the scattered clumps of yellow grass. Beyond the animals, a short beach surrendered to the tide, and a ghost moon hung in the day.

They named the tiger Sugar when Whistle adopted it, and they slept in a pile through the bitter winter, all of them in a single treehouse, wrapped around the cub. Since then Sugar had grown to his adult size and slept alone, often in the bush. Fish's body cramped in the tree, and he stretched as best he could. He had waited for hours, watching the grass where the tiger lay.

Any creature that passed Sugar's hide, the tiger would kill. It ran down gulls and clawed crabs from their holes. Feeling playful, Sugar flung armadillos ten feet into the air and caught them again, but where Sugar was at his most fantastic and terrible, Fish thought, was on the dunes, stalking horses.

In the year since Sugar began hunting, Fish had seen the half-wild ponies of Bomb Island kick and arch their backs when the tiger broke from cover to wrestle them by their necks and crush them to the sand or else ram them so they rolled with their hooves scrambling in the air. Next to Sugar, most of the thin island horses looked like dogs.

Twenty yards from Fish's tree, the foal dipped its head to pluck at the grass, and Sugar crept forward. This was as close as Fish had ever been. Even though they had raised Sugar from a cub, he always hunted alone. But the tiger was nearly within range of the foal, and it had given Fish no sign that it knew he was in the tree. Fish's hands began to sweat. He wished the horse would run.

Sugar might have been a concrete gargoyle, the way he lay over the sand, but the foal was saved. It was joined by a group of four healthy adults, and the horses climbed the dunes, walking in a mob.

Fish edged farther along the oak limb to watch Sugar slink backwards and melt away as the horses stomped into the grass. The tiger moved through the bramble at the forest's edge in silence, pouring his large body under limbs and into cover. When he passed beneath the branch where Fish lay, the boy saw the white-black pattern of his fur flash between the green saw palms. The purple needle points on the plant's leaf-tips barely rustled, they only swiveled around in small circles.

Soon Sugar had crossed back into the dunes, but now he was upwind of the horses and at their flank. Fish could see the tiger's face, eyes wide and body still. He was sorry for taking the binoculars from the side of Reef's bed, but he was glad he had them now.

Having lived first in a dank garage and then on the island, Sugar was a self-taught killer. The tiger must have thought he invented hunting when he approached again, creeping beneath the tideline and peeking at the horses over a lip of sand. Then he spooked a bird that, launching from the sticks it had been hunkered in, brought all the horses wheeling around. Sugar was caught with the sea at his back.

Sugar rushed the horses, snarling, but a dishwater stallion kicked him to the ground. He rolled once over the sand, then leapt back into the low surf. The water reached his chin. Small waves slapped his body and drenched his fur so that he looked small, just a knot of muscle.

The dishwater stallion stood with three brown mares between Sugar and dry land. They pushed the tiger deeper into the water and tried to flatten his head beneath their hooves.

Fish dropped from his tree and sprinted over the dunes. He shouted at the horses. "Hey! Yah! Getaway!" but they didn't turn. He snapped branches from a dead, white tree that was half buried in the sand and hurled them at the horses, then chunks of bark, then broken pieces of seashells, getting closer to the standoff until in desperation he tore the steel binoculars off of his neck and slung them into the ribs of a brown mare.

The horse turned to snap at Fish's arm, and Sugar slashed it across the neck, then escaped to the shore. Fish ran into the dunes, while behind him the mare cried and fled, and the rest of horses broke and ran down the beach with her.

Sugar's hips came to points with his wet fur pressed to his body. There was blood on the tiger's face. It welled out of a cut over his brow. "Hey, Sugar," Fish said. He kept his face to the tiger. He backed away slowly, shuffling towards the trees.

Sugar watched the horses run. He huffed and gagged salt water.

"Hey, Sugar. Easy."

This was the closest Fish had seen the tiger come to death, the first time he had seen it in real danger. When he charged the horses, Fish felt kindred to Sugar. Now, with the tiger shaking the water from its shoulders and leering at the distant horses, twitching his tail in frustration, Fish felt alone. He felt he should not be here.

"Easy, Sugar."

The tiger walked to the boy. Fish reached out his hand, and Sugar slid beneath it. White hair clung to his fingers. "Easy." Sugar pressed his head against Fish, and the boy stumbled. He bumped him again and swatted at his legs. Even play swats, with the tiger's claws tucked into its paws, would leave bruises. Sugar moved Fish like a toy. He wrapped his paws around the boy's leg and pulled him down.

"Sugar, stop!" Fish punched the tiger beneath its ear as hard as he could, but it didn't budge. He pulled at his leg, but Sugar had hold of him. He was alone on the beach. His family was a mile away at camp.

Fear got into Fish. He jerked his knee and screamed at the tiger. Sugar dragged him across the sand. When he felt the tiger's claws tear across his calf, Fish cried out and dug his fingers into Sugar's face. He felt the large eyeball squish beneath his thumb, and the cat recoiled.

As quick as he had come at Fish, the tiger drew away. The boy watched, stunned, as Sugar turned, shook his head, then sprinted down the beach on the last narrow strip of firm, wet sand not washed over by the tide. The celebrating horses had stopped to play and were high-stepping in and out of the surf. They didn't see the tiger racing towards them on the wind.

Sugar leapt from the sand and savaged the tall, dishwater stallion. He bit at its neck while his claws dug and kicked at its belly until the horse rolled to its side in the water and lost its throat. The other horses scattered and raced in twisting paths over the dunes and into the trees where they crashed like giant, graceless deer.

Fish limped to the woods. Even in the close cover of the ferns and palms, he felt exposed. His neck itched to turn, where he imagined Sugar crouched in the dark of the path behind him, just out of sight, but he never saw the tiger. He tripped through the skinny trails in silence.

The air clung to him. In the summer, Fish buzzed his hair close to the skin. He went without a shirt and wore a pair of faded blue trunks that were quick to dry. His skin was smooth and tanned. His limbs were slim. His stomach poked boyishly above his waistband, and a scarred mole grew from his upper lip. He dreamed of growing a thick mustache to cover the mole.

He had been born in Atlanta sometime in the last fourteen years. He never knew his father, and his mother, a woman named Sara, left him in Whistle's care. The Bomb Island commune that Whistle came from the city with had dwindled quickly, from fifteen, to ten, until only Whistle, the two men, and Fish were left.

He bore no resentment. For as long as he could remember, Whistle had been more of a mother to him than Sara. Like the horses, Fish loved the lonely wandering and deep quiet. He had lived on the island for seven years since his mother left.

Fish heard Whistle and Reef shouting in Whistle's treehouse when he neared the camp. He knew they had made love. For months now, they fought after they touched each other. Fish wondered if Nutzo was up there with them. He hadn't seen the old man all day.

Fish crept beneath the creaking treehouses and past the dead cook-fire to the shore, where he washed his bloody leg. Whistle and Reef were still fighting after he'd dressed the shallow cuts with ointment and gauze. He couldn't hear what Whistle was so angry about, or why Reef kept shouting out, "So? So?" He remembered what Whistle had told him about Sugar. She said he was a voyager, like all of them. "Learn from him," Whistle said. "He'll be learning from you."

Fish hadn't understood. "What will he learn?"

"That you're not afraid."

But the island had been Sugar's teacher. It had taught him that he was powerful and fearsome, and there were no lessons past that. All along the island's windward beach, the skeletons of hogs and ponies lay half-buried, tucked into the dunes. It might have been gruesome, but it was beautiful, how the driftwood curled next to the whole white bones.

TWO

In the morning, Fish crept from his treehouse. His leg felt tight and sore. The skin was bruised, and five long scratches spiraled from his knee to ankle, scabbing and sticking to the gauze wrap. The air, at least, was warm with biscuits.

"Have one," Whistle said. She was cross-legged by the coal bed with a book in her hands. Fish sat on a sandy cushion at her side.

Whistle's watch read six in the morning. They were due at Royals Marina in two hours to pick up their morning bomb tour. "How did it happen?" she asked, and Fish told her about the shore and the horses.

"Why did you follow him?"

"To watch him hunt."

"Did you run from him?"

"No."

"Can you work?"

"I can."

"You'll have to wear long pants."

"I know."

Fish peeled his bandages and walked to the shore to wash. Across the water, a green bulge of land on the horizon marked the Georgia mainland where Royals was. The salt water stung in the cuts Sugar made.

Fish filled his hands with fine brown sand and scrubbed his body. He had sweat through the night, still feeling the strength of the tiger crushing his leg like a phantom limb. Most nights he let a sheet of mesh screen hang over the opening to his treehouse to keep the mosquitos and flies out, but he had labored in the dark to affix the plank of wood he usually saved for bad weather. It could never have stopped Sugar, and it had made his treehouse stuffy and coffin-like, but he felt safer in the still, dead air.

"I don't think it's safe for us to be living with Sugar anymore," Fish said from the water.

"Let's talk about it later. After the tour." Whistle's brown nipples were pierced with small, wood-colored moons, and they swayed, side to side, as she pulled the brush through her long, silver hair by the coals.

Fish watched her breasts absently as he washed, thinking of the breasts that filled the colorful bathing suits of the tourist women that came on the bomb tours. He kept his face to the woodline and the water to his back. Then he flung himself into the sound and sank to the murky sand bottom and after ten seconds passed felt, finally, out of the tiger's sight.

"We need to talk about the binoculars," Whistle called when he surfaced.

"You know what happened," Fish said. Normally, Reef and Nutzo would be here, drinking coffee and smoking their first cigarettes. Fish felt a hole in his gut thinking of Reef, who kept the binoculars on his person most days in the large pocket of his shorts.

"How are you going to make it right?"

"I could have died."

Whistle stretched her legs on the sand. She leaned and reached and exhaled for a long time as she touched her toes. "Come help me."

Fish walked from the water to sit on the log behind the old woman. He gathered her hair in his hands and began to braid. He had, by now, woven Whistle's silver hair so many times that he didn't need to pay attention as his hands passed the strands over and under one another. His eyes were focused on the long scar that the braiding uncovered on Whistle's scalp. A line of raised purple that stretched from just above her right eyebrow to her ear. It had been made by a bullet.

When he finished Whistle's hair, Fish ran his finger along the edge of the scar. He kissed her head. "I'll find Reef a new pair of binoculars," he said. "With the tour money."

The Atomic Pleasure Cruise was a flat-faced, glass-bottomed boat with a blue sunroof and large silver engines bolted to its stern. Fish loved to sit in the swiveling, blue vinyl captain's chair and feel the roar of the engines through the throttle. He loved the wide, eagle-shaped wake that the boat left behind when it cut across the sound, ferrying the tourists to the far side of the island, where the bomb lay close to the shore.

The bomb was important to Royals, which was stranded on the

empty, marsh highway between Savannah and Jacksonville. And it was important to Whistle. The tours brought money, enough to keep life on the island comfortable. It was, briefly, important to the U.S. government, who sent divers in '85. Whatever the town expected—battleships that could lift the bomb from the bottom, or a pair of submarines to drag it away—it seemed like the uniformed men who came to see the bomb wanted it to disappear the natural way. Swallowed up and forgotten.

The news ran the story of the bomb like this: At two in the morning, February 5th, 1955, a fighter jet on a simulated recon mission collided with a heavy bomber on a simulated bombing run. The crew of the bomber jettisoned the atomic bomb over the dark water and performed an emergency landing in Savannah.

No one could agree if the bomb had its city-killing, plutonium core installed or merely a dummy core. The Air Force, whose bomb it was, said no. The Navy, who investigated the bomb in '85, said they didn't know. For Royals, that was good enough. Lights were installed around the bomb. Tours were organized. Shirts and hats were printed.

Royals Bomb is a Dud, the Savannah papers read, but on the billboards outside Royals a mushroom cloud swallowed a tiny cartoon town. Touch Death, the billboards said. Soon, suburban families were paying to "snorkel with the giant" and "brush eternity." Royals went from an unpaved crossroads to "The Nuclear Capital of the South!" which agreed with the town—to be known for something—even if the road remained unpaved.

Bomb aficionados began to appear. Fishermen who said they'd seen the planes collide and the bomb, like a smooth stone, skipping over the water. Crabbers who spoke of traps with colorless, ten-legged crabs. The town dug a new well, three miles inland. The newspaper held a forum.

People wanted to know: When the bomb exploded, how much would they be compensated for their homes and loved ones? Would the radiation lure migratory populations of fish? Whales? Would the subtle electromagnetic field of the bomb draw sharks from deep water? And if it did, would the atomic energy make the animals more aggressive or, some hypothesized, more passive? How much would someone pay to pet a bull shark?

"This was a disaster that we were spared," a pastor said. "Now it's an opportunity."

On the Atomic Pleasure Cruise, Fish eased the boat up Ottoman River, past the last no-wake sign and into the sound. He bumped the throttle and watched the tourists from the corner of his eye as they passed a bucket of pink snorkels and masks between themselves. A woman applied sunscreen to her children, then herself. She smoothed a quarter-sized dot of lotion into each arm, another for each leg, another for her chest. The woman met Fish's eye with a glance and he jerked the wheel, then overcorrected. The tourists hooted.

"How old is that boy?"

When they arrived at the bomb site, the usual questions began.

"Will the bomb go off?" a man asked.

"Yes," Whistle answered from her place next to the captain's chair. She kept her knees loose, rolling with the chop, sometimes resting her hand on Fish's shoulder. The tourists stilled to hear what she would say next. It wasn't difficult to get their attention. Most stared at her scar.

"When?" the man asked.

Whistle looked through the bottom of the Atomic Pleasure Cruise's hull, as if asking it: Is today the day? She wore a long white cover and looked sanctified. Like a body returned. It was ideal weather for bomb touring. The water played at green, shot through with light, and the shell of the bomb glinted on its sand bank, fading in and out of focus. The casings of the small electric lights, long dead and frosted with corrosion, circled the hulk.

"No one knows when it will explode," she said. "Inside the bomb is a capsule the size of a pill bottle, and inside that is a steel spring compressed by a wad of gauze, and against the gauze is a glass cylinder of acid that should have shattered when the bomb was dropped. The acid eats the gauze and the spring stretches out and triggers the explosion. But it hasn't happened."

"But it could at any time?" the man asked. "It hasn't been disarmed?"

"How would you disarm it?"

The man frowned. He made eyes with another man.

"It could be blown with a counterexplosive," the other man said. His short, angular hair gave him the look of a policeman emeritus. "They could use C4."

"Too close to town," Whistle said.

"Why hasn't it been removed?"

"The Navy came. The divers went down, but remember: Pill bottle. Acid. Spring. They decided to leave the bomb alone."

"How is this safe?" the sunscreen woman asked. "How is this legal?"

The tour murmured in agreement. They were all looking through the glass bottom now. The boat's rocking took on a hostile air. The wind turned cold. Tourists still struggling to wedge their feet into one-size flippers paused. They looked to the bare Atlantic.

Whistle and Fish had seen this before. Once, a man called the sheriff from his seat. "I'm trapped," he'd whispered into the phone.

"It's fine to worry," Whistle said. "But it won't blow today or tomorrow or this year or next. This bomb has been here fifty years. Hurricanes have come and gone. There was an earthquake in the '80s. Still, twice a week we come out here."

Fish noticed a boat in the distance. It was bounding down the length of the island, crashing through the waves. Rods and antennas protruded from its roof.

"I take it as a kindness," Whistle said. She was facing the tourists and hadn't seen the boat. "I take it as one of the great mercies in the world, at least in our world. Here is a bomb," she waved her hand down to the window in the hull and the tourists followed with their eyes. "When it was made, it was the single most powerful thing on the planet. Made to destroy capital cities in a second. Made to kill millions. But it refused. Look at it. It isn't damaged. It isn't sleeping, only resting on the sand. It could kill us all, but it won't. Mercy."

The tourists watched the bomb. A thin white coat of barnacles and brine stretched over its shell like the spots of an enormous cow. Peaceful, it seemed to lounge.

The boat in the distance grew closer and louder. It had a long orange hull and looked more like a racer than a fishing boat. An enormous white telephone number was stickered to the side of the hull beside an even larger graphic of a man's grinning face. It was the charter fisherman, Derbier. The tall, big-bellied man stood in the white-and-steel pilot's platform above the boat, shirtless and permanently lobstered by the sun. There was a man and two children on the boat, customers. Each of them wore Derbier's loud, orange hats. DERBIER! the hats read in block. Der-BEER!

Derbier's boat pulled alongside the Atomic Pleasure Cruise. "This happens," Whistle said. "Go ahead and prepare your snorkeling gear. Let's get the fins on, and I'll have a talk with our friend."

The tourists on both boats stared across the water at each other.

Derbier's fisherman cast his line over the side of the boat and began reeling.

"Piss off!" Fish said. Some of the tourists laughed nervously. Derbier snickered.

"Keep your mouth closed now," Whistle said very close to Fish's ear. Her face was drawn and lined. Her eyes, impassive gray.

"Mr. Derbier, this is an active tour. Our schedule is posted at the marina. Please leave the bomb site, and let's discuss this some other time."

Derbier held a jet of flame to his cigar until its tip glowed. "Is that John-Elvis's rig?" He nodded to the Atomic Pleasure Cruise. The man, Derbier's customer, cast again and reeled furiously until the line caught and the drag screamed.

"Ho now, Mr. Peter!" Derbier bounced on the deck of his boat like a fighter. "Fish on! Work him. Work him slow. Kids, get back there and watch your daddy work."

"That's a snag!" Fish shouted.

"Who says snag?" Derbier roared. Then he laughed. He beat his customer's back. "Your captain is scrappy, Ms. Whistle. Mr. Peter just wants to be a hero for his kids. Come on, Mr. Peter."

The man reeled against the snag until the rod tip bent and then pointed to an unmoving spot in the water. Then he wrestled and whipped the pole side to side, giggling.

"You need to leave," Whistle said.

Derbier threw up his hands. "What am I gonna do with Mr. Peter's whopper? What about the kids?" He wobbled on the steel platform, looking down on Whistle, who stood very still.

"Are you drunk?" someone on the Pleasure Cruise said.

"Has this woman, Whistle, told you she lives on this island? This island, which is a state bird sanctuary."

"Are you here to arrest me, Mr. Derbier?"

"And that on this sanctuary, she has imported all kinds of invasive species, which kill the native fish and wildlife. Kill them the same as this bomb, which, if you ask me, none of us ought to be near. Thing could blow any second."

Fish stood to whisper in Whistle's ear. "Let's just go."

"Sit down," Whistle said.

"And on the bird sanctuary," Derbier continued, walking around his deck with his hands on his stomach as he spoke, "she has imported an illegal, fully grown tiger."

"Goddamn!" Derbier's customer said. "Is that true?"

"That is true," Derbier said. "Think of the poor birds. Think of us. She's hiding the tiger there illegally. It could swim out and kill any one of us, Mr. Peter."

"It looks like Mr. Peter is finished," Whistle said. The man had left his rod leaning against the chrome railing of Derbier's boat. The tight line held it upright. "Please leave."

Derbier's lip curled when he saw the abandoned rod. "Mr. Peter, you mean to tell me that fish fell asleep?"

"What?"

"Man, shut up."

The customer made a wet, coughing laugh and sat in the shade on deck with his children.

Derbier chewed his smoke. He started the twin outboard engines. "Fine then," he said and tossed wet plug of his cigar onto the deck of the Atomic Pleasure Cruise. It landed on the glass bottom and stuck at the end of a short brown smear. "Bye, bitch," Derbier shouted. He gunned the big engines and sped off, turning wildly and throwing a strange wake that rocked the irate tourists in their seats.

"Why didn't you do something?" one of the tourists asked.

"What do we tell the police?"

"Did anyone save the number from the side of his boat?"

Whistle walked to the center of the Atomic Pleasure Cruise. She picked up the cigar stub and dropped it into a hanging trash bag. "Ladies and gentlemen," she said, "I am sorry you were witness to that display, but the weather is with us, and if you're willing, I believe we can still have a fine time on the water today."

"We should have rammed him," Fish said.

"We would like to go back to the dock," a young man said. Two boys sat with him, both younger than Fish. One was crying and the other stared with red, puffy eyes.

"Does that boy have a license? Where are his parents?" It was the woman Fish had watched lotion herself.

"I can see that Mr. Derbier has upset our morning," Whistle said. "If I may, let's pause for a moment."

"Can we just snorkel?"

"If I may, there is still time to complete our tour and to return to the dock. I am only suggesting we take fifteen seconds to clear our minds of anger and that we decide what we will do next from a place of clarity."

The boat was silent. Whistle closed her eyes. "Thank you," she said. In twos and threes, the tourists bowed their heads, part of a strange prayer.

In the fifteen seconds that the tourists, Whistle, and Fish sat in silence, a breeze arrived from the ocean. The anchor chain knocked against the deck and lifted off again. A wild turkey howled in the woods.

Fish kept his eyes open and watched the long, ocean-facing beach of the island. They were too far south to see the place Sugar had hunted last night. Fish was sweating inside of his black sweatpants and his scratches burned. He looked through the floor of the boat to the bomb, which sat like a giant, gray grouper beneath them, and he wished it had done something. He wished it had loosed a small token of its power on Derbier.

Fish had swum with the bomb for years, and he had never felt any sort of energy or life coming from it. When he slid his hands under the guidance flaps at its tail, his palms came back black with an oily gunk that took days to wash off. He believed the bomb was dead.

"Thank you," Whistle said into the silence. "Now, who would like to see a very large, very merciful, very beautiful bomb?"

When the tour returned to the dock two hours later, the tourists were placid, sun-drained, and wobble-legged. They thanked Whistle for what they had seen. They apologized for her harassment. They tipped generously. Whistle thanked them all, then waved them away. That was her magic too. Second-chance magic.

Fish braced himself in the captain's chair. He had already rinsed and scrubbed the deck of the boat. It was noon and a scorcher. New, dark puddles formed on the dock around the tourists' feet, then lightened and disappeared.

"I was just sticking up for us," Fish said when Whistle returned from seeing the tourists off. Her tiny body seem to loom over him. Her shadow shrunk to a small circle around her wrinkled, brown feet.

"You did what you wanted to do, and in doing so, you undermined my authority in front of Derbier, which is not sticking up for us and did not help."

"What did you do?"

"I told him, calmly, what he needed to do, which was to leave."

"And when he didn't."

"I insisted he did."

"And what if he hadn't left?"

"He left."

Fish groaned. He sagged his arms as if carrying a great weight. He jumped from the boat. His shirt and sweatpants dragged in the water, but he swam until his head ached and his outstretched fingers touched mud. Fish looked up at the dark picture frame shape that the glass-bottom boat made. A square of light surrounded by the rectangular hull. He could see the blob that was Whistle, still standing on the glass in front of the place he'd leapt from. He watched her sit down.

Then something crashed into the water. A body. A second later, strong arms grabbed Fish around the middle and pulled him to the surface.

"Get off me!" Fish said. He coughed and sucked for air.

"You get off," Reef said. "Losing my specs."

Reef pulled himself onto the Atomic Pleasure Cruise. He was shirtless and wore his cutoff fatigues. For years he had grown his long rusty hair, which he kept in dreadlocks and tied in a braid that reached the base of his neck. The sides of his scalp were shaved clean. He picked up the silver aviator sunglasses he liked from the dock and returned them to his face. His body was strong. He might have been forty or twenty-five. "I would have given them to you if you'd asked," he said.

Whistle climbed the steel ramp that led to the boat lift and the marina store. Likely to talk with John-Elvis, Fish thought. He wondered what she would do about Derbier. If she would do anything at all.

"I'm sorry," Fish said. He peeled off the oversized black shirt that was stuck to his body.

"Let's see the leg," Reef said. He sucked his teeth when Fish showed him the scratches. "That's not good."

"No," Fish said.

"What did Whistle say?"

"That we'd talk about it later."

Sugar was wild, but Whistle still sunned with him on the beach. Some nights the tiger slept with her. "She'd never leave him," Fish said.

"Well she'll have to do something."

"She's too merciful for that."

"What'd you say? What are you talking about?"

"She let Derbier walk all over us. He called her a bitch."

Reef laughed. "You think a lady who's been shot in the head cares about a blowhard like that? That guy's a joke."

"How is he a joke? He was in a bigger boat. He's a big guy. He was threatening our group. People that had paid."

"But did he do anything?"

"He called her a bitch."

Reef pulled a towel from a compartment on the boat and dabbed the water from his head. "But did he do anything?"

"He threw his cigar at us."

"Sounds serious."

"It was!"

"Don't let it get to you," Reef said. "Be like Whistle."

"Can I see that towel?" Fish asked. Reef was drying his legs and stepping into his sandals.

"Why?"

"To dry off."

"I thought you were working today. Specs cost twenty dollars in the marina store. Plus tax."

"I just worked," Fish said.

"You just pissed off your boss, is what you did. But that's okay, I got you a new job." Reef opened another compartment on the boat and brought out the thin, steel scraping tool. He pointed to a tall, green sailboat at the end of the dock. "This one has been sitting in the water since December. Got barnacle buds and sea moss."

The sailboat was massive. It would take Fish all day to scrape its bottom clean. Likely two days. "That's twenty dollars?"

"No, it's fifty, but I'll handle the money. You just get us started today." Reef dropped the scraper in the captain's seat and climbed off the boat.

"Where will you be?" Fish called after him.

"Darlin's. Find me later."

THREE

The sailboat needs a scratch like a dog rolled over. Under the hull, Fish could barely see. The water around the island was cold and fresh; it roared in from the Atlantic in great currents and it left the next day. The water at the marina was slow; it had been trapped in the coastal, saltmarsh rivers for days, boiling in the shallow creeks that marbled the marsh. Fish tread water beside the boat at dock. Large, rainbow oil spots drifted beneath his nose. Men chatted at the top of the steel ramp that led to the marina store. The air stank with gasoline.

Fish's hands blurred through the green water in front of his face, hacking and scraping the sailboat's white hull. Sunlight bullied its way through the load of mud suspended in the water. Mud so thick, when he surfaced after an hour of working in the murk, a mud beard clung to the thin white hairs on his face.

He sat on the dock, resting and flexing his muscles into the sailboat's windowed portholes. He imagined walking to town wearing his new beard. Handsome and his lip mole-free. His man-dick swinging in his pants. Older, taller, broader.

He scrubbed the dirt off his face and drank from the water hose that lay on the dock, then he fitted his mask onto his face and lowered himself back into the still-tide river. He breathed through the pink Atomic Pleasure Cruise snorkel. He slid his palms over the bottom of the sailboat and pushed the scraper where he felt a burr or the brush of a saltwater plant. Normally this work was done out of the water. With a power washer and in minutes. Cleaning the boat like this, he reasoned, what could the owner expect?

Fish's arms ached. The cuts on his leg stung. He had ditched the sweatpants and swam in his boxer shorts. He clung to the side of the boat with one arm, and swung his other with the scraper, his head above the waterline, and his eyes closed in exertion. His mouth was open and he panted as he rammed the edge of the scraper into the lip of a barnacle fastened to the hull. The slamming became rhythmic. He thought of the woman lotioning herself on the tour. He wondered if she had come from far off. He marveled at the way she had spread the lotion. He remembered it was smooth as cream.

The hinges of the dock squealed behind his head, but he did not open his eyes. He was thinking of the woman and ramming the scraper against the burr. When he sucked air through the snorkel, it drew warm water and he gagged, then vomited where he swam. What he had sucked through the snorkel was rank. It burned his throat, all through his nose. He ripped off his mask to see Jonathan with his dick in his hand, still shaking it. Another high school kid was there too, filming with a handheld.

"Fuck you!" Fish shouted. He rinsed his mouth and spat. He remembered Jonathan. He remembered that he drove a small, muddy fishing boat of his own. He knew Jonathan's father wore suits on the water and that he held his son by the hair when they fought. Jonathan had told him once. He had approached Fish weeks ago with the same handheld he had today. He'd said he wanted to interview him. He wanted to know about the bomb, and where Fish slept, and what he ate every day, and was that mole on his face contagious?

Jonathan had filmed the interview with his off hand and looked, seriously, into the camera after each of Fish's answers. Shaking his head and saying, "Isn't that something, folks?"

"He wants to fuck you, Jonathan!" the high school kid said from behind the camera. "I think that means he liked it!"

Jonathan stuffed his dick back into his fly. "Figures."

Fish hauled himself out of the water, but Jonathan kicked him back in with the heel of his boot. His ears rang. He clung to the side of the sailboat. He raised his fist numbly and saw that he had lost the scraper.

"Of course he wants to fuck me," he heard Jonathan say. "He's a dirty fucking freak. I know he fucks the bomb witch up her old ass."

"I'm going to chicken-fuck your ears," Fish screamed. He pulled himself to the deck of the sailboat. He tried not to think about his boxers clinging to his dick. The cameraman cheered him on. Fish snatched a metal folding chair off the sailboat's deck and threw it at Jonathan's back as he posed for the teen with the handheld, but the chair fell short and only skidded over the dock.

Jonathan picked up the chair. "What were you going to do with this?"

"I'm going to beat you with that."

Jonathan looked shocked. He jumped back. Then he smiled and flipped the chair into the water on the other side of the dock, where it disappeared. "Bye," he said, and walked away with his cameraman.

"Chicken-shit bitches," Fish yelled from the sailboat, but the teens kept walking. He had scraped his leg getting onto the boat in a hurry, and it bled onto the deck in thin, bending streams. He caught another tang of the piss in his mouth and gagged. "Fuck."

John-Elvis walked out of his store, hollering for the boys to tell him their names and their daddies' names. The boys laughed. They lifted their middle fingers into the air.

"Who told you to touch that boat?" John-Elvis shouted down to Fish.

"Reef."

"Who the hell is Reef?"

"It's for Whistle."

The old man's skin was reddish and hung from his jaw like a wattle. "Well fuck if I know anything then!" He stomped back into the marina store to his baseball game.

"Fuck!" Fish's blood stained a white rug left, impossibly, on the ship deck. "Fuck!" He dove from the dock and swam to the bottom of the river, where the mud was thickest and the sun barely shone. He felt around for the metal folding chair. It had looked expensive. He had read the boat's name, *Deluvia*, painted on its back. His hands passed over broken cinderblocks and the slick skeletons of tree limbs. A brown ray glided beneath him. He surfaced, dove again. The chair was gone. He imagined its wide back catching the water like wind and blowing far away from the dock, through the river and into the Atlantic.

In the captain's chair on the Atomic Pleasure Cruise, Fish bandaged his leg and drank three bottled waters. He brooded on having to tell John-Elvis he'd lost the chair. He debated whether or not he would tell Reef what Jonathan did, and he wondered what Jonathan did with his videos. He remembered all the words he'd said while the camera was watching. Chicken-fuck. He heard himself say it again. He hoped he hadn't looked scared.

He wished Nutzo was with him. The old man was quiet. Quieter than Whistle and without so many ideas to share. In the summer, Fish spent long days pushing Nutzo's log raft, his "gondola," through the tidal rivers of the island's southern marsh, fishing for flounder in a few, scattered holes that stayed cool. Nutzo liked to fish from beneath the gondola's tarp awning, reclining on the cushion of a salvaged boat seat. He had thin, surgical scars over this throat and spoke in an airy rasp. When Fish had a question he didn't want to ask Whistle, Nutzo told him what he wanted to know.

"What age does your penis stop growing?" Fish asked him once.

"When mystery dies."

"How big should your penis be?"

"As big as it can."

Fish hadn't told Nutzo about Jonathan's interview and how it ended, but he wished he had. He knew the old man wouldn't tell Whistle or Reef about what had happened. He would know what Fish should do now and what Jonathan wanted to know when he asked Fish if he was "intact."

They had been at the end of the dock, hidden behind a block-shaped houseboat, and Jonathan had the handheld up to his eye. "Intact. You know," he said. "What does your dick look like? Did they cut you on the island?"

"No one cut me."

"You wouldn't remember. Just show me."

Fish pulled his trunks down.

"Oh shit," Jonathan said. "It isn't cut at all. It looks like a fucking tentacle." He aimed the handheld at Fish's penis and pointed his finger at the round, wrinkled end. "That shit rolls back when you get hard?"

"I guess."

"Does it help you jack off better?"

"I don't know."

Jonathan snatched at Fish's penis and testicles. He gripped them in his hand.

"Shit! Fuck. Stop," Fish said, but Jonathan only squeezed. It felt like the air was being crushed from his lungs. When Fish fell to the dock, Jonathan stooped down to keep his hold. He kept pointing the handheld at his hand squeezing Fish and then dragging the shot up to the younger boy's red face.

"Do you jack off?" Jonathan squeezed him. "Don't lie."

"No."

Jonathan balled his hand into a fist on Fish's genitals. "Tell the truth. I will know."

Fish lay his head on the dock. "No. I don't know."

Jonathan laughed. "Got a tiger by the toe now, son!" He howled. "What's your real name?"

"Stop."

Jonathan squeezed him again, then snatched his hand away as urine sprayed onto the front of his shirt. "Fucking disgusting!"

Fish had lain on the dock, sweating. He'd felt dizzy. He became aware of the sun's glare. His piss pooled around him and felt cold on his legs. He remembered what Whistle told him about vultures. How they can't sweat and, so, piss and shit down the sides of their legs to cool down.

"Fucking freak."

✳

Darlin lived in Sea Wall, which was a grid of small, brick houses and mobile homes set off the dirt road. It was the only named neighborhood in Royals, which was itself barely a place without a post office or even a gas station. Just the two antique pumps that John-Elvis kept to fuel the boats.

Fish climbed the steel ramp from the dock and passed a crowd celebrating the close of a fishing tournament. A silver-haired man read the weights of kingfish from the back of a truck to scattered cheers from the people who watched. Two young men in the truck with the silver-haired man lifted each long, striped fish high in the air and turned them slowly, like champion belts, for the crowd. The expensive off-shore fishing boats, a few plastered with sponsor stickers, had all been hauled out of the water, trailered, and rinsed. Most were filled with crews of middle-aged men, who sat like warlords in their longships and clapped seriously for the winners of each category.

Fish crossed the dirt road and passed into the grass field that was Sea Wall. Over the years, he had been in several of the homes, helping Reef or Nutzo with yard work or repairs. Any odd jobs John-Elvis passed to Whistle. He climbed the concrete stairs to Darlin's porch, opened the screen door, and knocked against the warped white door behind it. The knocks sounded muffled against the soft wood. He saw Reef's sandals slid beneath a wicker chair. He listened for footsteps and heard nothing and grew uneasy, standing at the door with his back exposed to the houses around Darlin's. He never knew which were occupied.

When Fish walked around to the side of the house and pressed his ear beneath Darlin's bedroom window, he expected to hear her bedframe grinding rhythmically against the wall, but it was quiet inside. Then he heard Reef laughing. Fish pressed himself to the brick wall and snuck the short way to the back of Darlin's house, where there was a small, attached screen porch.

Hidden by the screen and the hanging vines of pothos, Reef and Darlin were bathing in a claw-foot tub. Fish heard gentle splashes and the occasional smack of falling water on the concrete floor. They weren't talking, only making sounds. From around the corner, it sounded to Fish like they were murmuring into one another. He imagined them sitting, face-to-face, in the cast-iron tub, leaning deep into one another's mouths and making the hushed, hopeful moans he heard. They pleaded. They said Thank you, thank you. They splashed and then stilled.

"What are you doing?"

Fish screamed and leapt away from the wall.

A brown-haired girl with a bright green cast had appeared at his side. "Who are you?"

Fish heard a body stand in the tub and, without answering the girl or giving her a second look, ran from Darlin's yard to the next, ducking behind a shed and then running again to get behind the next house and the next. An old woman lifted her watering can at him as he sprinted, as best he could with his hurt leg, past her. He didn't stop until he reached the woods at the neighborhood's edge, where he hunkered against a U-shaped tree.

"What are you, a pervert? Are you hurt?" It was the girl with the cast. She was standing on the other side of the tree, panting.

"I'm fine."

"Well, are you hiding from me? You want to come around here and talk? I've got mace."

Fish leaned around the tree to see her. She was maybe fifteen years old. Definitely older than him. She had a small black can of mace pointed at his head. Her skin was pale, her eyes dark. In the late afternoon, they looked black.

"I'm not dangerous," Fish said. He raised his hands. "You're the one chasing me."

"You want to sign my cast?" She held it up. Swirling names covered the green "L" molded to her arm.

"I guess."

"Well then come out from behind that tree."

Fish hesitated. "How do I know you're not going to mace me?"

"Because if I wanted to, I would have while you ran or, like, right now. I sprayed it on accident once. I mean, the safety came off and I tapped the trigger, just a little squirt came out. Everybody in the restaurant started coughing. They all had to leave."

"Did you start coughing?"

"Yeah. My eyes teared up."

"How is that a good weapon?"

"You want me to mace you and find out? Like this. Away from you." She held the can with her outstretched arm and pretended to spray it. "Hose them in the eyes and run."

Fish adjusted his wet, sagging sweatpants and tightened their drawstring. He wished for the oversized black shirt that he had left, wet, on the floor of the boat, and for the second time in the day, he felt naked. He knew his stomach poked and his ribs showed. At least his leg was covered. He worried over the mole on his face. "Okay, I'm coming out," he said, and limped from behind the tree with his hands raised. "Do you have a pen or something? Can you not point that at me?"

The girl slid the can of mace into the pocket of her jean shorts and produced a marker. "Come over here." She held the marker out. When he reached her, she slapped his face with it.

"What the hell?"

"Don't creep."

"I wasn't creeping. That's my brother."

"Reef is your brother?"

"Yeah," he said. "How do you know Reef? Who are you?"

The girl looked him over. Fish was sure she was thinking the same questions Jonathan had asked in his interview. He could tell she was wondering if he knew how to read or if he ever brushed his teeth. He checked his breath against his hand. It only smelled like sweat.

"I'm Celia," the girl said. She shook his hand with her good arm. She surrendered the marker as if it were a gun.

"I'm Fish."

"Write it up. Or draw something. Do whatever." The only blank space left was on the underside of Celia's arm. Elbow to wrist.

Fish paused with the marker tip hovering over the lime-colored weave of the cast. Sweat rolled into his eye, and he felt that the bandages on his leg were wet and out of place. "Can we sit?"

They sat on the hardy, sharp grass, and Celia propped her arm on her knee. Fish drew the hook of a dorsal fin, a torpedo body, a muscled tail. Minutes passed to the squeaking of the marker. As he drew, he relaxed. His eyes followed the shape of the dolphin.

"You a serious artist type?" she asked.

"No."

"You draw?"

"Yeah." Fish concentrated on the dolphin's back. He wanted it bent like he'd seen on the island. A bottlenose dolphin in a perfect semicircle, leaping a wave and entering the water again.

"Why don't I know you," she said, "if you're Reef's brother. One of the mysterious island elves."

"What?"

"That's what I call you. I saw the remodel Reef did on Darlin's porch. And the bathroom. She said the older guy fixed her car. Which kind of elf are you? Cabinets?"

"I mostly do the yards."

"How do you know Darlin?"

"We're just friends. Where do you go to school?"

"I'm homeschooled."

"On the island?"

He wasn't supposed to say that he lived on the island. Even if people knew. Especially if they knew. But she knew Darlin, and she knew about Reef and Nutzo. He wondered what else she knew. "Do you have any other markers?"

"No," she said. "Is there really a tiger out there? On the island?"

"I don't know. Why don't I know you?"

"You don't know if there's a tiger living on Bomb Island, where you also live?"

The marker was running dry, but he wanted to see a fish racing ahead of the dolphin, cutting the water. He pressed down harder, squeezing out the last bit of ink. He could see the white circle of Celia's face in his periphery, staring at him while he hovered over her cast. He had been drawing for so long that, even though he didn't know her, he had slid his body close to hers. With his off hand, he held her casted arm upright while he drew. He looked at her fingers sticking from the top of the cast in a tuft of gauze, pink and half-bent, and he thought of how it would feel to lay his fingertips against hers.

"I don't want to talk about that stuff," Fish said.

Celia looked annoyed. "Why not? It's interesting. I'm sure it's hot and all. No A/C. But your life sounds insane! I mean, you're like, basically an emancipated minor at like fourteen."

"What is your life like?"

Celia plucked at piece of hair stuck to her face. The sun was nearly down, but the heat clung to them. "It's fine. I'm just here for a couple weeks. Staying with my dad. I live in Savannah."

"Come to see the bomb?"

"No. Are you going to ask how I broke my arm?"

"No."

They sat in silence. Celia's breasts reminded Fish of a rabbit he had once seen Sugar hunt. The tiger had flushed the rabbit from its cover, but the rabbit was quick. It ran to the thick sand of the dunes and, quickly, it dug a hole and dove inside. Sugar went the other way, and the rabbit lived. Fish had watched the place it hid under, which pulsed with its frantic breathing. Possibly, Fish thought, it was the first time this behavior was seen by human eyes. It looked like a small patch of living sand.

The gnats had found them by then and lifted from the ground in a swarm to wriggle in the hair of their arms and legs. They scratched their scalps and resmoothed their hair. Fish concentrated on the crude stippling that shadowed the dolphin's back. He hung a moon behind it. He scratched out delicate, many-sided shapes for stars.

"Jesus, dude. You could have just written your name."

"This is better," Fish said. He nodded for her to look.

"Well damn." Celia held the cast up to her face. She craned her head to see how far the drawing stretched. "This is quality stuff. You do a lot of animals?"

"I guess."

"How about these?" She turned her leg to show a flying saucer on the back of her calf, pricked into the skin with ink. Tapped out in dots, sort of. The whole saucer and the levitation beam too. A dotted smiley face was caught in the beam, getting drawn into the ship.

"Or these?" She turned the other leg, and showed the long, alien arm with cracked fingernails reaching down her calf. It looked like it was about to grab her ankle with its strange, long-fingered hand. "These are some of mine."

"Pretty serious," he said. He was still looking at the alien arm on Celia's leg—behind her knee, where it started and the alien's forearm ended in a shred of flesh and bone. At the end of the bone, there was script: Noli me tangere. His eyes followed Celia's leg to the place it disappeared into her shorts.

"It's from a poem," Celia said.

"What?"

"Never mind."

"Right, the poem," Fish said. He was proud of the dolphin he had drawn, but it looked doodle-ish next to Celia's alien tattoos, even the blurry and misshapen ones. They shouted Permanent and Adult. "How did you do those?"

"These," Celia pointed to the blurry dotted tattoos, "I did with a needle and pen in middle school, and this big boy," she gestured to the alien arm, "I did with a gun."

"A gun?"

"Tattoo gun. I made it myself."

"Where did you learn that?"

"Where did you learn to sneak up on people having sex?"

Fish's blood froze. "I was just looking for Reef."

"Well you found him. Why'd you stay?"

"I don't know. Because I wanted to."

"Wanted to what?"

Why wouldn't she quit? Fish felt a ripple of anger in his embarrassment. She wasn't much older than him, but she acted like she knew everything, and had known for years. She would think he was a child. He wanted her to think he was like her. "I wanted to know how it works."

"Sex?"

"Yeah."

Celia stood from the grass and wiped off her legs, she reached out her hand to help Fish up. "There's nothing to know. Penis in vagina. End of story."

"You know that much?"

"I know what everybody knows, but if you want to know about it, you should just ask someone. Like, what do you want to know? You get one question."

She seemed annoyed. It was hard to think of a question with her staring at his mole. All that came was the memory of Whistle, Reef, and Nutzo locked together in the treehouse. Behind the burlap curtain, Reef's hands were beneath Whistle's legs, holding them while he pushed against her. Nutzo held Whistle and kissed her lips. His hand covered one of her breasts. They wouldn't hurt each other, but their faces were pinched. Then Whistle had shouted, and Reef lunged to rip the curtain closed.

"When should you start?" Fish asked.

"That's your question?" She covered her eyes. She blew a bunch of air through her lips so it sounded like a long fart. Then her brow bunched up in wrinkles. He had made her angry. "You don't want to know what it tastes like?"

She meant girl sex parts, he knew. "No."

Celia squinted to see his expression in the near dark. Eyes wide and avoiding her own. Mouth ajar. Dried mud on his cheek. Cracked lips.

"No," Fish said. Her light eyes were sweeping over his face, looking for the lie. He was short enough that she could see over his head and into the woods behind him. The setting sun was cutting through the trees.

"Alright," Celia said. "Good. Start anytime then. Whenever you find yourself a nice pal. And stay out of people's windows." She waved her good arm in a wide arc as she turned away and walked back towards the houses. "Later."

What had she wanted him to ask? Fish thought. Would she tell Darlin where he'd been? He racked his brain for what to say, how to make her stay. "How did you break your arm?"

"Why do you want to know?"

"I signed the cast."

Celia laughed. "I have to go. You really want to know about my arm? There's a party next week. Friday. At that house," Celia pointed to the dark shape of a brick house, identical to Darlin's except for white truck parked in front of it. "You got it?"

"What time?"

"Dark, dude."

FOUR

A week passed. On the island, Fish healed and thought of Celia and tattoos. He decided a vagina would smell and taste like the top of someone's head after they had worn a hat all day because of the hair that covered the vagina and the fact that it was, generally, covered by clothing. In the dark of his treehouse, Fish tested his theory on the sweaty crease of his elbow. The taste was salty, in a light sort of way. It didn't linger like the tang of blood.

Nutzo was still gone. There were only so many ways that he could have gotten off the island. They didn't have any powered boats besides the Atomic Pleasure Cruise. Fish saw the gondola beached on its mudbank. It hadn't moved since he and Nutzo dragged it onto the shore more than a week ago. Fish imagined the old man wading into the water and swimming to shore, or to the next island down the coast. Why would he do that?

Reef thought that Nutzo simply wandered into the woods. "He does this all the time," he said, but no one could remember a time when Nutzo left for a week without telling someone. "He might be at his brother's place in Atlanta. He just didn't want to make a scene leaving."

After three days of searching and waiting with no sign, Whistle took the boat to the marina to use the phone. The number she had for Nutzo's brother was disconnected. She returned to the island after dark. Fish hoped that her taking so long on shore meant that she had found Nutzo. Maybe he had tried to hitch back to Atlanta, but gotten stopped along the way. Whistle came home alone and secluded herself in her treehouse. Over a cold dinner, she said she had called a dozen numbers at the marina and even made a report to the police.

"I hope he's happy," Reef kept saying. "I just hope he's pleased."

Fish had never heard Nutzo talk about his brother or wanting to leave. He tried to order and replay the day he'd last seen Nutzo. It was the morning he had followed Sugar hunting. Nutzo returned to camp with a stringer of trout, and Fish had watched him filet the fish. They left the guts in the usual place, deep in the woods, where Sugar or the raccoons or something would find them before the day was out. He was humming, Fish remembered. He wanted to paint. He wanted to stretch canvas while Fish and Whistle toured the bomb, but the canvas was still in its roll on the end of Nutzo's cot.

"What if Sugar got him?"

"No," Reef said. "We'd have found something."

"He could have dragged him up a tree," Fish said, even though he had never seen Sugar do this. An image of the old man, caught in the branches of an oak with the meat of his legs stripped like a trout filet pressed itself on Fish. The nightmare came from his encyclopedia. A dark photograph of a leopard with a gazelle.

"He's still alive. Probably eating a cheeseburger right now."

Fish thought of horses with open necks and faces of Nutzo and how some mornings, after Sugar made a kill, the soft sand told the story. The deep cuts of the horses' hooves and the wide prints of the tiger. The dark blood dried in clumps.

On one of their long, meandering searches for Nutzo, Fish saw that the body of the dishwater stallion had disappeared. The tide had carried it off. While he walked behind Reef through the afternoon, Fish dreamed of the horse's body running over the ocean floor.

They saw Sugar infrequently and always from a distance. Whistle walked into the woods after dark to call him, singing his name like she had his whole life, but the tiger never showed, and Fish was glad.

When they gathered at the camp to share a dinner of oranges, black beans, and saltines, Fish kept his back to the water and his eyes on the trees.

The camp felt abandoned without Nutzo, as quiet as he was. Most nights, he only said a few words. Whistle ate her orange and read a book, but Fish hadn't seen her turn a page. Reef finished his meal quickly, cleaned his bowl, and climbed into Whistle's treehouse.

"I'm going to stay down here," Whistle said.

"All night?" Reef asked.

"I don't know," she said. She sounded small. Her hair was down and cast a shadow on her face. Her scar was hidden under cords of greasy strands. She hadn't been washing. Gathered in a quilt on the sand, she might have been someone's grandmother and not a priestess at all. One of the soft, mortal women that sat with small children on their tours.

Reef laughed. "Suit yourself." Fish heard him pushing the bedding and books over the wood floor, looking for something inside the shelter with a small light he clipped to the bill of his hat. "You got the keys?"

"I have them here."

Reef came back to the fire. He stood over Whistle where she read. "I need to get out of here for the night."

Whistle kept the smooth silver key of the Atomic Pleasure Cruise on a leather thong around her neck. She took it off and handed it to Reef, but when he took hold of the key, Whistle kept the strap clinched in her hand. "I would like you to stay."

Reef winced.

"Please stay here tonight."

The last story Sara told Fish was about Whistle and how she'd saved their lives and become their mother. It was an old story. There was a fire in their apartment building in Atlanta, which Fish remembered as waves of black smoke on a white ceiling. He and his mother were trapped in their room. He always imagined it was Whistle who broke the door down with an axe to free them, though Sara said she only told the firefighters where to go. They lived with Whistle from then on. Maybe she was an angel, Sara said.

The other people who lived with Whistle said the same. She had saved them all from something. Drownings and hangings and bad marriages and the wrong kinds of drugs. They believed she couldn't be killed and got their proof when a bullet struck her head.

Whistle denied the miracle. After she healed, she sold her house in Atlanta and moved with her new family to Royals. She knew things, like how to dig a well and what vegetables to grow. The people on Bomb Island fished and foraged what they could and bought what they couldn't from the marina store. Whistle knew how to live like that—not off the land, but gently tucked inside of it.

Fish sat beside the coals at camp, thinking of how this had once been just a secondary cook fire. The dinners those first years on the island had been celebrations. He struggled to remember the names of all the men and women who had left. They never spoke of them. He didn't want it to be like that with Nutzo.

Reef left for Darlin's on the glass-bottom boat. Whistle brought her reed mat down from the treehouse and lay on the shore. Fish stacked deadfall and driftwood on the bed of coals until the flames reached three feet tall, then he cleared the sand around the fire of sticks and shoes and lay on the beach next to Whistle. The stars seemed to dip into the water. Venus was a dime.

Whistle's eyes were closed. Her brow was wrinkled. From time to time, she rubbed her eyes. "Bring me some water, Fish?"

He went and poured from the plastic jug. When he came back, Whistle was sitting upright, stretching. He set the water down next to her mat. He picked at the flake of a scab on his healing leg. "I got invited to a party," he said.

"Who invited you?"

"A girl I met in Royals." The way Whistle laughed made Fish's stomach burn. "What's funny?"

"Nothing, baby. Which girl?"

"Celia."

"Celia who?"

"I don't know."

"Well, what kind of party is it?"

"I don't know. A party-party." He wasn't asking for permission. What did Celia and the party have to do with Whistle? "I'll just need the key tomorrow is all," he said.

"Is that right?"

"Yes."

"I'll be searching tomorrow. Isn't that more important?"

"We would have found something by now."

Whistle's lip curled. "Is that what Reef said?"

"It makes sense," Fish said.

"Do you remember when you burnt your foot?"

They had made a large fire of green wood and buried the coals in wet sand. Two days later, the coals were hot enough to make the skin peel from Fish's toes when he, mistakenly, stepped on the place. The pain had been intense. Balloon blisters covered the bottoms of his feet, and he was unable to walk. Every day, Nutzo had helped him to the cold water to soak his feet while Reef and Whistle tended the camp and led tours.

"I remember," Fish said. "I love Nutzo. I just don't think he's here."

"I'm not talking about Nutzo being nice to you. I told you that day, I had a dream you were hurt. I said to wear your shoes. Do you remember this?"

"No."

"Well I did. And I've been sitting on this mat since dinner, dreaming, and I know that Nutzo is alive on this island. He didn't leave. You know he wouldn't do that. Don't let Reef tell you otherwise. He's just scared."

"Who's scared? Reef? What would he be scared of?"

"That Nutzo may be hurt," she said.

For the first time, Whistle seemed unsure. He could tell she didn't believe what she was saying. She looked like she had survived a blast. "What about the others?" Fish asked. "What about Sara?"

"Fish, you're a smart boy, but you don't know what you're talking about this time," Whistle said. "Those people, Sara, they were some of my best friends, but they weren't ready to live like we live. It wasn't for them. They recognized that and went their own way. You know Nutzo loves it here."

"He doesn't love Sugar." The old man had always kept his distance from the tiger. The mornings he woke in Whistle's treehouse and found the tiger sleeping on the woman's other side, he'd lie frozen in bed until Whistle made the tiger leave. He had asked her more than once to find another home for Sugar. "Maybe he left because you wouldn't get rid of Sugar."

Whistle looked away from him. He could tell she was upset, but his stomach was still tight with anger. "Why did you laugh when I said I met a girl?"

"It surprised me. I didn't know you made a friend on Royals. I haven't met any girls named Celia."

"What, you think I made it up?"

"Did you?"

Fish howled. "No! All kinds of things happen that you don't know about, and they're still real."

Whistle was silent. She looked over the water towards Royals.

Fish thought he heard a boat's motor, but there was nothing. The wind moaned in the trees. Fish watched the pine tops nod in unison and regretted what he had said, but the heat in his stomach, the tension in his shoulders told him "Go on." The night had come on in full, but the sand glowed.

"I spoke with John-Elvis about what Derbier did. He won't bother us anymore."

"How do you know that?"

"I just told you."

John-Elvis had stood, slack-armed after Jonathan and his cameraman had flipped him the bird. "What is he going to do?"

"I don't know, exactly. He might refuse to rent him docking space. If he can't dock here, he'll move his fishing business somewhere else. He's only been here a few years."

Fish laughed. "If I were Derbier, and someone tried to refuse my docking space, I'd just blow them off. John-Elvis would do what? Call the police and ask them to put a paper ticket on the boat?"

"They could tow it."

Fish waved his hand. "I wish Sugar would gut that guy."

"Who is this talking? Where is this coming from? That's not what we do."

"Well," Fish said. He realized he was looking for something to hurt her with, but he didn't know why. "We is getting smaller every day."

"Baby, we are going to find Nutzo."

"It's not about Nutzo. I don't care about Nutzo."

"I don't believe that."

"It's not even about him." He began to shout. "It's about you not keeping us safe. Keeping us together. It's about you not doing anything when somebody hurts us."

"What are you talking about, baby?"

"I'm not your baby!" Fish stood and walked from the beach. It was the first time he had yelled at her in years. What had it been about the last time? He had wanted to swim farther into the ocean, deeper than she said was safe. A week later, a riptide carried Reef a hundred yards from the beach and held him there. If Nutzo hadn't been with him on the beach, if they hadn't had a boat, he would have died.

Fish sat by the fire, reduced now to a pile of flickering log-ends. He watched the shape of Whistle's head and shoulders by the water. Behind her, the gibbous moon looked like a smashed thumb.

Sugar appeared across the fire, lying where Whistle sat each morning. He wasn't sleeping. His eyes were on Fish. He might have been there all along.

"Hey, Sugar," Fish said. He sat very still. The ladder to his tree-house was only a few feet away, but if the tiger wanted, he would never make it there. "Whistle," he said.

"Oh hey, Sugarman," Whistle said. The tiger lifted his head and made a deep clicking sound, a chuff, and Whistle sat at his side. She stroked his massive head and scratched his shoulders. "It's alright now," she said, but when Fish stood to go, the tiger tensed. It growled.

"Whistle," Fish said. He was frozen in a half squat. His knees shook.

"You need to calm down, Fish," Whistle said. Her voice was level and serious. "Calm down, sweetheart. Sit by the fire."

"I don't want to." Fish stepped away from the fire and Sugar stood. He watched Fish with wide eyes. It was the same way he looked at gulls on the beach.

"Lay down, Sugar," Whistle said. "Easy." She pushed on the tiger's rump, but it wouldn't sit. It only watched the boy. "Fish," she said. "You need to sit down now. He can feel that you're upset."

"I don't want to sit with him," Fish said. He began to cry. He took another step from the fire, and the tiger walked towards him. "Get back!" He kicked sand, but Sugar kept on. "Whistle?" She had disappeared from the fire. He was alone. Fish took another step backwards, and his heel caught on a log. He fell.

Sugar closed on the boy and swiped the air over his head, asking to play.

"Get out of here!" Fish sat up and flung more sand. "Go!" Sugar lunged for him, and Fish kicked him squarely in the face. He felt the wet nose crunch.

The tiger turned its long body away and stepped into the brush. Fish strained to see the blur of it in the undergrowth, but the tiger was invisible. The boy walked backwards to the treehouse ladder, never taking his eyes from the place he saw Sugar last.

"Fish?" Whistle called from the campfire.

"I'm here." He could see the shape of her on the sand beneath him. She was holding something. It gleamed. It clicked in her hands.

"Do you want me to come up there with you?"

"Is that a gun?"

"It is."

"I thought you didn't believe in guns."

"Do you want me to come up?"

"No," Fish said. "Goodnight."

"Goodnight."

In the morning, Fish woke to Reef grilling sausage and eggs in his underwear over an iron griddle at the cook fire. Whistle was sleeping in. On the top rung of Fish's ladder, she'd left a necklace. A twine cord, weighted by a piece of bone-white driftwood, twisted into a teardrop. She must have made it while he slept.

"Where did you go?"

"Nosey," Reef said.

"Darlin's?"

"Quit." His eyes were sunken and dark. "The cat came by." He pointed to the torn-up space where Sugar had pushed Fish over the sand. There were tiger prints all over the sand.

"Sure," Fish said.

"Sure. You tiger-proof now?"

"I told him to leave, and he went."

Reef handed Fish a plate. "He came at you again?"

"It wasn't that bad. I kicked sand at him. Look." Fish lifted his leg in the air. The scratches Sugar left there had flaked and peeled and only thin, purple lines remained now.

"Very nice tiger wound, bud." Reef grabbed Fish by the ankle and hauled him into the air. He dragged the boy over the soft sand, shouting, "Yes, ma'am, this is a genuine tiger strike on a genuine human leg."

Fish laughed. "Put me down!"

"No need to worry about your safety. He's an all-star sand kicker. Cham-peen defender when it comes to large jungle beasts."

Fish tried to kick loose, and Reef heaved him into the air. "Fisher-man!"

They walked human-lawnmower-style over the beach until Fish rolled and dug his shoulder into the sand and played dead.

Reef dropped the boy's legs and sat down next to him on the shore. "How would you feel about going back to Atlanta?" he said. "I've got people there still. Maybe we'll find Nutzo."

Fish glanced at Whistle's treehouse. Its flap door was still closed. He wondered if Sugar was up there with her right now. If he hadn't dragged her off.

"Would Whistle come?"

"You know how she is."

"Yeah." Fish dug his hands into the sand.

"It's not safe for us here now. You remember this?" Reef pointed to a mass of old scars on his foot and ankle. "And this?" He held up his forearm, where an S-shaped indentation bent the muscle.

"She knows it's bad. Maybe she'll send him away."

"She'd never do that."

When the conversation had come up in the past, Whistle deflected. "Why were you with him during mealtime? Why were you playing rough?" And if the wound was serious—Reef had nearly lost his arm—she devolved. She shrieked at the tiger. She ran Sugar into the woods, slamming steel pots over her head, but she would sit with him on the dunes a few days later. She talked to him. She read to him. "I'm making progress," she would say at camp.

"You don't have to decide right now, but I want you to think about it. We could have a good time," he said. "You like Darlin, yeah?"

Fish liked the watermelon tea that Darlin sometimes made when they visited, usually to fix something in her house. Reef and Darlin left the TV on for him when they slipped into the back room. Once, while he pruned bushes in her lawn, Darlin asked him how many other women Reef had. Besides that, she had never spoken to him alone. He didn't know if he could love her like family.

"Will you take me to a party tonight on Royals? Celia invited me."

"Who's Celia?"

"Darlin's friend."

"And she's a girl-kid?"

Fish held up his hand, a little higher than his head. He imagined Celia materializing beneath his palm, sitting on the beach with him and Reef in her bright green cast. She'd have to keep it dry, he remembered from a book he'd read. "A little older than me."

"You want that? Probably be a bunch of kids there. I don't know where she'll find a bunch of kids in Royals, but there might be a crowd of them."

"I want to go. I'm invited."

"You like this girl?"

"I don't know. She's cool."

"Alright," Reef said. He was thinking something over. "Let's talk about what we're wearing."

FIVE

y an hour after dark, the party had spilled from the small
brick house that Celia pointed to. The front yard was filled
with white pickup trucks. Teens in collared shirts and cutoff shorts stood in and around the truckbeds drinking from cool-
ers and packing their lips. Country music played. Three older girls
danced like children in the yard. A group of sun-damaged adults
kept to the back, sitting in a tight circle of lawn chairs. Inside the
house, the groups mixed.

An enormous teenage boy with cowboy boots and a baby face sat
on a cooler in the center of the living room. When someone wanted
a drink, he would raise himself to a squat over the cooler and pass the
ladle between his legs. A woman Whistle's age lounged on the couch
with her eyes closed, bobbing her head to the music that played.
One person flipped playing cards in a line on the floor and ten others

shouted and shot liquor. A young ship captain and his girlfriend necked in the kitchen, while boys ate lunchmeat from the refrigerator and a drunk girl cried on a stool, drinking wine from a bowl.

"I'll get us something," Reef said. He kept his aviators on inside the house. He and Darlin wore jeans and matching black shirts, Reef's very tight with the sleeves rolled up and hers loose and comfortable. Both of the shirts were Darlin's.

They looked good together, Fish thought. Darlin's soft features and long black hair seemed to envelop Reef's sharp, rangy build when they stood with their arms wrapped around one another. They laughed easily. He considered what it would be like to live with them somewhere far away. He might be happy like that. He didn't remember much about Atlanta. Only the fire and a few loose ends, half memories made of images that had lost their context. Tortoise shell-patterned cement on the walls of a tunnel. Brake lights. A red steel jungle gym and hot, stinking asphalt turning a shower of rain to steam.

They had showered and dressed at Darlin's house. Fish wore his newest black athletic shorts and a green tank top of Darlin's that fit him like a dress. "It'll show off your arms," Reef said. Fish tried to hide the mole on his lip, but Darlin's makeup only drew attention.

It had been Reef's idea that Fish should shave the sides of his head with a razor, leaving a buzzed brown mohawk. "They won't be thinking about your face," he said. "They'll be thinking, 'Damn, that guy looks cool.'"

Darlin's house had once belonged to her grandparents and it was still filled with their things. Reef and Fish sampled her grandfather's cologne collection, settling for a green bottle that read "Sportsman." It smelled like pepper and smoke.

"That's confident," Darlin said.

Beneath the tank top, Fish wore the necklace with the teardrop pendant that Whistle had made him. In his dreams he gave it to Celia, and she kissed him on the mouth. "That was something," Fish would say in his dreams. "You're something too," she might say back. He had never been invited to a party before.

At the party, Fish searched for Celia. There were only two bedrooms in the place. The door to the first was locked. When he pressed his ear to wood, Fish could hear a young couple arguing, but the girl's voice was high and nasally and not like Celia's. In the second bedroom, what looked like the master, twelve school-aged boys had pushed the king-size bed to the side and were wrestling on the floor, most of them shirtless. A boy with bloody scratches on his sweaty, white skin had Jonathan in a headlock on the floor. Everyone was shouting. Jonathan had his eyes squeezed shut, wrenching at the arm around his neck.

Fish stepped out of the room, then back inside. He thought he had seen something. The boys had piled their shirts by the closet door. On top of a short dresser was a pile of watches and Jonathan's silver handheld.

Fish moved behind the circle of boys still shouting for Jonathan to slam the other boy against the wall, to flip him over, to do something. When he picked up the handheld a pimply boy with red hair backed into him. The boys in the circle were turning on one another, snatching up ankles and knees and slamming each other to the hardwood floor.

The red-haired boy, about Fish's age, flashed him a smile and reached for his head. "You want to go?"

"What's the capital of Mexico?" Fish asked. He raised the handheld.

The boy grew serious and straightened from his fighting stance. "Who are you?" Then a tall blond boy spear tackled him into the closet door. The wood panel snapped under the weight and crushed in on rows of shirts and piles of shoes. The rest of the boys laughed. One of them crumpled a lampshade against the wall. Another threw an ashtray from the nightstand.

On the floor, Jonathan's face was purpling. The boy who held him, bored that no one was watching him anymore, dropped Jonathan and heaved the king-size mattress off of its bedframe. He began to drag it from the room.

Fish slipped into the hallway with the handheld. He saw Reef and Darlin in the living room sitting with the card players, but he ducked out the front door before they noticed him. He had to turn his shoulders sideways to fit between the teens gathered around the trucks. Someone spit near his bare feet. "Hey, kid." But Fish ran from the yard and into the woods. He didn't stop until he was ten yards into the brush with his back against the trunk of a tree. He stared at the camera in his hands. He should smash it against the tree. He wanted it to be gone, but he also wanted to be sure his video was on the camera. It had been weeks since Jonathan interviewed him.

"Fish?" It was Reef at the edge of the woods.

He left the camera at the base of the tree. "I'm here."

"What are you doing?" Reef's face was sweating. His sunglasses hung from the front of his shirt.

"Partying."

"In the woods? Come on. You want to go back to D's place?"

"Not yet," he said. They could see Darlin's house from where they stood. It was just on the other side of the dirt road that cut Sea Wall into four sections. Darlin was crossing the road, headed towards her front porch with a drink in each hand.

"A party like that, it's just a matter of time until the sheriff shows. You don't want to be there when that happens."

"I know," Fish said.

"I mean it."

"I know."

"Well, what do you think?"

"About what?"

"About it's your first party, and you're hiding in the woods. What happened in there?"

"Just kid stuff."

"What's that mean?"

"Don't worry about it," Fish said. He touched the smooth shaved sides of his head. "I'm cool."

He found Celia in a pull-through garage in the backyard, sitting on a riding lawnmower and drinking a beer with two teenage boys. Her blue lipstick sparkled. She wore ripped black jeans and a t-shirt with a gorilla on its front. There were more signatures on her cast than the last time he had seen her.

"Oh my god," she said. "It's the Fish guy. And your hair looks rad!"

"Thanks."

One of the boys standing beside Celia nodded in his direction. "What's up." They were working on something. One of them held a flashlight, and the other had his arm laid flat on a cluttered workbench.

Celia sprang from the lawnmower chair and held her cast in the air. "This is the dude! Look at this shit!" She pointed to the dolphin drawing. Someone had signed their name on its belly. The sky Fish had drawn was buried in scrawl.

"We seen it. You draw a lot?"

"I used to."

"Come check this shit out." At the workbench, one of the boys was stabbing a hornet into the forearm of the other with a needle. The hornet was drawn on the underside of the arm and the boy with the needle followed the lines, dipping the needle into the ink of a disassembled ballpoint pen and then sticking it into the other boy's skin. He moved quickly, poking along the guidelines, while the other boy drank his beer and watched.

"Your real name is Fish?" the boy with the needle asked. His eyes were focused on the hornet.

"Yep."

The boy nodded. "I'm Mason."

"Lester," the boy getting tattooed said. He set down his beer to shake Fish's hand. Both boys had thin brown mustaches on their lips. Their hair reached to the bottom of their necks.

"This tattoo is going to be a mess," Celia whispered in Fish's ear. Her breath was sour, but it made his head feel woozy. She dug a warm beer from an open cardboard box next to the lawnmower and passed it to him. He had drunk with Reef before and swallowed a mouthful dutifully. He hated beer.

"Cee, the flashlight," Mason said.

"Have Lester hold it," Celia said, and the boy who was getting the tattoo took up the light. Then she led Fish to a dusty lawn chair next to the lawnmower and the two of them sat and watched the boy with the needle prick Lester's arm. Blood and ink pooled where the hornet was.

"I thought you said you had a gun." Fish said.

"They wanted to do it this way," she said. She pulled the tattoo gun from a backpack on the ground. It looked like a mechanical pencil with a tumor. Electrical tape wound around the top of the pen and held batteries in place. Celia flicked her thumb over a tiny plastic switch and the device began to hum. "Hold it," she said.

The top of the pen felt heavy and awkward in his hand, but it vibrated sweetly.

"Try it on this," Celia said. She pulled a lemon from the beer box and then a small container of black ink. "Just dip and rip."

"Rip?" With the tattoo gun on, the needle shot in and out of the pencil tip in a blur.

"You'll see."

"I like to go side to side," the boy with the needle said. "Makes the ink go in better."

Fish noticed then that the boy's legs were covered in the same kind of blotted, blurry shapes that Celia had. Homemade tattoos. He wet the needle and touched it to the lemon. The large pores of the fruit filled with ink that smeared when he wiped with the cotton rag Celia gave him. He began to draw a sleeping dog curled around the woody stem-place where the lemon had been attached to its tree.

"A dolphin!" Celia guessed.

"Nope." He leaned to catch the light from a bare bulb that hung on a cord from the ceiling.

"You go to Benedict?" Lester asked.

Fish didn't know what that meant. "No," he said.

"Cool."

He had drawn for as long as he could remember, but he had never used a machine. Fish watched in amazement as the pen hummed over the lemon tip and the dog appeared, laced into the bright yellow skin. He felt Celia's eyes on him, watching the tip of the tattoo gun pinched between his fingers.

"You're a natural," she said.

Lester and Mason leaned from the table to see the lemon, and Fish held it out to them. "Do mine like that," Lester said.

"I like stick-and-poke better, but that's nice," Mason said.

"I'll sell you that gun for fifty bucks," Celia said.

"Really?"

"Nah," Celia said and laughed. "This my baby boy."

In the yard, the boy with scratches on his back had hauled the king-size onto the grass. The pack of shirtless boys from the bedroom hung around the mattress, lifting each other into the air and crashing to the pillow top.

"Is this your house?" Fish asked.

"Not even close," Celia said.

The boy with scratches walked into the pull-through garage. "Any gas?"

Celia pointed to a small, red canister on top of a shelf, and the boy took it back to the mattress.

"You cool with that?" Mason asked.

"Why should I care?"

"Shitgoddamnit, Mason!" Lester pulled his arm off the workbench. The skin on the inside of his arm was red and bled, amazingly, from the point of the hornet's stinger. He snatched a blue rag from the ground and pressed it to his arm. "You fucking stabbed me."

"It was his first," Mason explained.

"Oh," Fish said.

"What the fuck should that matter?" Lester kept lifting the rag and looking at the tattoo. "Probably gonna get infected."

"You have to bleed your first time," Mason said. "Everyone does it."

"Who stabbed you?" Celia asked him.

Mason lifted his shirt to show an indistinguishable tattoo that began to the left of his belly button and stretched past his waist-band. He tensed his stomach muscles. "I did it myself."

"Alright, dude," Celia said. She handed Lester one of the beers.

"I heard the cops might come soon," Fish said. He had finished his dog and was inking tiny planets into the fruit. Ringed Saturn and oceaned Earth. The Eastern Seaboard appeared. Phallic Florida and the long Georgia coast. He felt like he could say anything to Celia while she watched him draw.

"Who told you that?"

"Reef."

"What, he call the police?"

There was a loud whooshing and shouts from the yard. The king-size mattress was a raft of flame. Human shapes danced around the tall fire. People flooded out of the house to watch. The yard factions came together. Pinch-faced old-timers stood with sweating teens. Rare, green flames tongued the spaces between the springs, and the party rejoiced. Some held their hands in the air.

"You live around here?" Mason asked Celia. "You want a ride?"

"You're leaving now?"

Fish wondered what it would mean if Celia went with the boys. Would it mean she didn't like him? He worried that he didn't have a car to offer Celia a ride in, and, at the same time, he realized that he wanted to offer her a ride. He knew she lived somewhere in Sea Wall. He imagined walking with her between the short houses. If the moon were fuller, he could show her the burial mound in the woods.

"We could get some food," Mason said.

"No thanks," Celia said.

"We could all go together."

"Nah."

"Later days." The boys walked towards the trucks parked in the yard. Fish could hear them bickering after they had walked a few yards.

"Whose house is this?" Fish asked. He gave the tattoo gun back to Celia.

"An asshole's."

"It's getting trashed."

"Good." Celia slumped back in the lawnmower's seat and cradled her cast against her stomach. She rested her legs on the steering wheel and crossed her ankles in the air. There was a small pile of beer cans scattered around the floor of the garage. She studied the inked lemon.

The beer had Fish feeling fuzzy and warm. In Lester's seat, he found the plastic chair was wet with sweat. He wondered how much pain the boy had been in. "Thanks for inviting me," he said. "This is for you." He held the driftwood necklace out to Celia.

Celia took the white, wooden tear. She held it very close to her face. "This is amazing," she said. "Holy shit." She handed it back to Fish. "But I can't take this."

"Why not?"

"I don't know you very well."

"We just met."

Celia set the necklace on the hood of the mower. "It's very cool. I just don't do gifts."

"Why not?"

"I just don't. I don't like keeping up with it. Who owes who."

"It's not like that. My mom made it for free." Mom was easier than explaining who Whistle was to him.

"Your mom made this?" Celia picked the necklace back up and held it in her palm. The twine was braided through the wood and tied in an intricate knot. "It's beautiful, but I don't do gifts. Plus, she wouldn't like if you gave it away." She handed it back to Fish. "Put it on," she said, and he slipped it over his head.

"Yeah, that's something. Mom's necklace. Buzzcut and shit. Like a wild man turned loose."

"You look wild," Fish said. The bright, orange light coming from the mattress, made Celia's blue lips electric and threw shadows across her cheeks. She turned her head to belch. He had never kissed anyone on the lips before, and he worried his mole would brush her face if he tried now.

"Give me one question," Celia said. "I gave you one."

Fish's head began to sweat. He wished he had a truck instead of an island. He wondered what she had meant when she said he looked like a wild man. Wild like dumb? Like dirty? "Sure," he said. "That's fair."

"It's fair!" Celia threw her beer onto a high shelf loaded with rusted coffee cans. She was drunk.

"Nothing about my family."

"Okay," she said seriously, nodding. "That's cool. Tell me about the horses."

"That's not a question."

"What is, tell me about the horses, Alex?"

"What?"

Celia shook her head. "How many of them are there?"

"A lot."

"I've seen them on the beaches sometimes. From a boat."

"Then you know." He wondered if she had seen the skeletons in the dunes. She must have. Who knows what she had seen if she'd been watching from the water. It wasn't uncommon for boats to ride around the island when the weather was good. When the boats were in sight, Fish and the others kept to the trees. "Do you ride or something?" He had hoped she would ask about him.

"No," she said. "I just think they're beautiful. Their khaki coats and furry feet. I think it's awful. They're trapped. And they destroy the turtle nests."

"They get by. They're tough. And smart."

"I'm going to get them off the island one day."

"How?"

Celia sighed. "They'll have to tranquilize them. Move them out west or to some land. They'll figure it out."

"Who's they?" Fish imagined the helicopters and armed men he had once seen in a movie about Vietnam sweeping the island for the horses. Shooting them down and putting them in bags to haul away. "Who would do something like that?"

"Well, like, the State of Georgia. I could write some letters. Maybe get a petition signed. Send it to someone in Atlanta. It could happen. I know you guys are out there or not or whatever, but that's who owns the island. My dad talks about it sometimes."

"I've never seen anyone like that out there. State people."

"Would they make you leave?" Celia asked.

"I don't know."

"Is the old woman that does the bomb tours your mom? She made the necklace?"

Fish hesitated. He had said no family stuff, but she wanted to know about him. She was looking at him, leaning off the lawn-mower in his direction. "She made the necklace," he said.

"You do school out there?"

"I can't talk about that stuff," he said. What could he tell her about himself? he thought. He could feel his window to speak to her, to know her, closing. His scalp itched.

In the yard, the crowd moved to make way for a Jeep covered in black cargo webbing to pull close to the fire. The stereo bumped slow, rhythmic bass. Somebody climbed onto the matte fender and danced. Then another person. The music played, and the Jeep bounced.

"How did you break your arm?" Fish asked.

Celia laughed. "Look at this guy! Remembering shit." She was still watching the flames. "It got slammed in a door."

"Your arm?"

"Are you going to start being dumb now? Yes, my arm."

"How did it happen?"

"I told my dad I was leaving. I slammed the door. He snatched my arm back inside."

"Shit."

"Yeah."

"So he didn't mean it?"

"What do you mean, 'mean it'?"

"Like, he didn't mean to hurt you."

"Does it matter?"

Fish didn't know what to say to that. Celia's voice was as hard as Whistle's. Indisputable. "Do you think it matters?"

"No, Fish. Shit. Plant your feet. Does it matter that my drunk-ass dad didn't mean to break my arm?"

"Yes."

"Why?"

"If he meant to break it, he's dangerous. If he didn't mean it, he made a mistake. That means he won't do it again."

Celia clawed for another beer with her off hand. "Don't take this the wrong way, but you sound like you're about ten years old, dude. What? Don't look some sad-sack puppy. Listen to me. This is going to help you. He's dangerous no matter what. How much shit does someone have to break before you get that? Before people get that. Do you know what a zero tolerance policy means?"

"Yeah."

"It's means no bullshit. No controlling people. No having to live with the motherfucker who breaks your arm in a door."

"I'm sorry that happened," Fish said.

"Yeah, me too, but like, fuck it. Cast is off in six weeks. And when my dad gets back and sees this"—she pointed to the burning king-size with her beer—"I'll be back in Savannah by morning."

"Shit. This is your dad's house?"

"He'll either kill me or send me back, but he won't touch me. It's okay." There were tears in Celia's eyes.

"Do you know these people?"

"Some of them. It's not hard to throw a party."

An orange truck whipped into the front yard, blaring its horn. From the open window, Derbier raised a shotgun and fired into the air. People screamed and scattered. "The sheriff is on the way. Get the fuck off my property!"

Derbier looked to Fish like the feral version of the charter fisherman who had ruined the Atomic Pleasure Cruise's tour. His lips were drawn back to show large, yellow teeth. He raced the engine of the truck. He smashed his fist against the horn. Run to Darlin's, Fish thought, but his head was buzzing. His ears rang from the shotgun blasts. He was paralyzed.

"You should go," Celia said calmly. She sat up straight in the lawnmower chair and swayed. She took several deep breaths. The bones of her fist jutted white around her steel can of mace.

"We should both go."

"No, I need him to know it was me."

Derbier stepped onto the grass without his gun and ran into the house, shouting. The few people left in the house burst through the front door, laughing and stumbling to their trucks or into the darkness. "Celia!" he shouted. "Where are you?"

"Tell him it was you on the phone!" Fish said.

"I'm out here, asshole!" Celia shouted. "Really, get out of here," she said to Fish. Her words were slurred. "Go!"

Maybe a dozen people were still in the backyard when Derbier erupted from the back of the house and ran to the garage.

"Easy," an older man said. He stepped into Derbier's path, and Derbier shoved him away.

"Get in the house!" Derbier shouted.

"No," Celia said. She stepped from the lawnmower and pointed the mace at Derbier.

Fish stood behind her. He had been in a daze since he had seen the impossible orange truck. He remembered the sneer on Derbier's face when he called Whistle a bitch. It was like he was haunting him, Fish thought. Coming at him all the time. Trying to break him down. To destroy him.

"Who is that?" Derbier shouted. "Come here." He lunged at Celia, and a stream of orange liquid sprayed into his face, dropping him. Derbier pawed at his eyes, moaning on the ground.

"Who's a dumb bitch now, dumb bitch?" Celia screamed.

It was hard for Fish to keep his eyes open. His vision blurred with tears. The air stuck in his throat. He pulled at Celia's arm, and she wheeled around and pointed the mace at him.

"Get off me!"

Derbier stood and lurched for Celia, but he smashed his knee into the front of the lawnmower and fell again.

"Oh shit, dude!" a man said from the yard. Maybe a dozen people had come back to watch Derbier roll on the ground.

Derbier struggled to stand, he threw his arm at the laughter coming from the yard. "Get out of here!"

What had Whistle said? Fish thought. He could feel his blood slamming in his ears. She said she had handled Derbier. That he wouldn't be around anymore. Well, he was around. He was around and breaking arms. Fish crossed the garage and kicked the kneeling man, hard, in the throat.

Derbier flopped over on his back. His face was a puffed mass of tears and teeth with slits for eyes. He was opening and closing his mouth, holding his throat and gasping.

Fish stomped on the mound of his gut.

"Oh hell yeah," someone shouted.

Fish kicked Derbier in the ribs, and his toes went numb. He kicked him again, and Derbier rolled to his side, covering his head with his hands. "Get gone! Homeless bitch!" Fish screamed. Someone grabbed his arm.

"Stop!" It was Celia. "It's done."

The dark bricks of Derbier's house lit up as a police car rolled through the shallow ditch and into the yard.

"Let's go!" Fish said. When he pulled at Celia's good arm, she pulled it back.

"Get off me. Go where?"

"Away!"

Celia wobbled on her feet. She looked to Derbier, who was rasping on the ground, then at the police. "Okay, okay," she said. "Shit! Wait!" She ran into the house.

"Where are you going?" Fish ducked behind a tall toolbox in the garage.

A moment later, Celia appeared from the house with her backpack. She sprinted through the yard and the deputies called for her to stop. They trained their flashlights on her. Then a group of three boys ran from the house, and the police shifted their lights, shouting commands, but never leaving their car.

Celia and Fish ran out the back of Derbier's garage and into the woods. Fish weaved between skinny pines and crashed through sticker bushes until he found the narrow trail. He led Celia by the hand and snatched the handheld from where he'd left it as they raced towards Darlin's house under the cover of the trees.

SIX

An ambulance sped through Sea Wall with its sirens off. Fish and Reef had their faces pressed to the large window in Darlin's living room. They could still see the blue lights of the cruiser still flashing at Derbier's.

"They only do that when someone's dead," Fish said.

"No, it's just late. The cops would have called the ambulance when they saw he'd been maced."

"Really?"

"They would call. Especially if he was beaten. Those rides are expensive too, so he can suck on that." Reef stepped from the window and put his hand on the back of Fish's neck. "It's done now."

"Yeah." It didn't feel done to Fish. He was still reeling with adrenaline. His breath fogged the window. He was waiting for Derbier's monstrous face to appear in the dark.

"What's with the camera?" Reef asked.

Fish had put the handheld inside of his backpack when they returned to Darlin's, even before he told Reef about Derbier and the fight. "I just found it at the party."

"You took it?"

"Yeah," Fish said. He had never stolen before. He didn't know what Reef would do, but he didn't think he would take the camera.

"You don't need to steal."

"Reef," Darlin said from the couch. She was rubbing Celia's shoulders. "Help me with some drinks."

Fish and Celia sat in silence on the couch while Reef and Darlin argued in the kitchen. Before they'd reached Darlin's porch Celia had vomited. She'd rinsed her face and changed into one of Darlin's sweatshirts. "I can't believe that happened," she said. Her lipstick was smudged. "I can't believe I did that."

"What are you talking about?" Fish said. "You said it yourself. Zero tolerance. Someone tries to break you down, you stop them."

"Why did you kick him?"

"He was dangerous."

"He was down."

"He called my mom a bitch."

"What?"

"He broke your arm!"

"Look, I don't care. You can kick him all day. I'm just saying, I had it. You didn't have to get involved."

"I don't care about that. I'm not scared."

"No," Celia said. Her hands were in fists. "Like, it wasn't your business."

"I just told you why it was my business. It was about my mom."

"Right," she said. "Whatever."

Reef and Darlin came back into the den carrying iced water in coffee mugs. "Celia," Darlin said. "You are more than welcome to stay here, but I can't deal with the police right now because of legal stuff with the house. So you'd have to say you stayed someplace else if they ask."

"Totally," Celia said.

"Stay on the island," Fish said. "We've got room."

Celia shook her head. "No. I'll call my mom and tell her what happened. She'll pick me up in the morning. Is that cool, D?"

"Of course," Darlin said. She motioned to a white cordless phone on a table. In the years since Celia had been forced to visit her father in Royals, she had stayed at Darlin's a handful of times.

Reef sat on the couch next to Fish. "What do you think about Atlanta? We could leave tonight. What do you think about that? You kick the shit out of that asshole, and we just blow town. Outlaw shit."

"And leave Whistle?"

"We'll call her when we get there. Think about it, if you're gone and I'm gone, she'll split. She'll come to us in Atlanta. Maybe Nutz will be there."

But Fish wasn't listening. He was watching Celia walk to the cordless phone and dial her mother's phone number into the green, glowing digits. "Come to the island with us," he said again.

"Fish, no," Reef said.

"We have the room. Celia needs a place to lie low just like us. Derbier is crazy."

"He won't be able to do anything to me in Savannah," Celia said. "He won't do anything to me here. I'm okay."

Fish felt sure that if Celia went to Savannah, he would never see her again. "You could learn about the horses. I could show you. See what they're eating and how much."

"Fish, we aren't going back to the island," Reef said.

"I am not leaving Whistle!"

Someone stomped onto Darlin's porch. A boot slammed into the door and it crashed into the room, held to its frame by a thick brass chain. Derbier's wrecked face stuck through the gap. "Send my daughter out right now!"

"Get out of here!" Celia shouted.

Derbier stepped back and lifted his shotgun. He fired into the door, and splinters and gun smoke filled the air.

"Go!" Reef shouted. He flung open the back door. "Go to the boat!"

The four of them ran from the house and across the road. Behind them, they heard shouting voices, and the wail of sirens. Angry male voices shouting and shouting back. They skidded down the dock's ramp, gripping the steel railing.

Reef leapt into the Atomic Pleasure Cruise and started the engine. He shouted for Fish to untie the boat from the dock while he helped Celia step on board. "Get in," he said to Darlin. "We'll figure it out."

"I don't want to be there with her," Darlin said.

Reef hung his head. "Your door is shot open. That means cops. We'll figure it out, I promise. I love you. Just get in the boat."

Darlin stepped onto the deck, and Reef steered the Atomic Pleasure Cruise away from the dock and into the river. "Hang on." He pressed the throttle, and the outboard gurgled, then roared. The wake of their leaving ground the other boats against the dock and made their bumper floats scream.

The river was flat. The cold air bit their ears. Celia and Fish sat opposite each other with the boat's glass bottom between them, both of them staring through the black window. From his side, Fish saw Celia's reflection in the bottom of the hull. She closed her eyes when she noticed he was watching her.

Darlin stood behind Reef at the captain's chair and spoke into his ear over the engine. Fish couldn't hear what they said. They were, both of them, staring flat-faced at water ahead of the boat. They kissed quickly, and Darlin sat next to Celia on the cushioned bench seat.

The boat left the mainland marsh. It flashed past mud banks and the little specks of dry land that supported small huddles of dark tress. It moved from the salt river to the dark expanse of the sound, where the water was rougher. Even a boat as wide as the Atomic Pleasure Cruise, which glided on two steel pontoons, had to rock and beat its way over the small waves that the wind kicked up. Reef piloted them through it all.

Fish's foot hurt, and he remembered that he had been in a fight. He remembered feeling the edge of Derbier's large belt buckle when he had kicked him, and looked down to see a cut across the top of his bare foot. The blood had dried. Celia was looking north, where the horizon glowed with the lights of Savannah, far away. Ahead, the sky was dark blue over the island. It would have been easy to believe, Fish thought, that they were soaring off the edge of the earth.

When they were close enough that they could see the silver marshes of Bomb Island, Reef pulled back on the throttle. The motor and wind quieted. "Celia," he said. "If you want to go back to the mainland, I'll take you right now. We can go up the river, and you can call your mom from a pay phone I know. We'll find change along the way. I know a couple of—"

"It's okay," Celia said, quietly. "Just keep going. I want to stay wherever D is."

"I love you, sweetheart," Darlin said.

Celia's shoulders rocked. She was balled up, with her feet on the bench seat and her face buried in her arms. When she cried, the sound was strained.

"You are going to be okay, Celia," Darlin said. "No matter what."

"Okay," Reef said. He turned the boat into the mouth of a narrow creek and through its bends. The marsh was drowned in high tide, reduced to thin green fingertips that poked from the water. When he found the place on the shore where they would dock, he sucked his teeth.

Whistle stood at the tying tree with an oil lamp in her hand, lifted over her head. Her hair stretched out in the wind. It seemed twice the length of her body. When she saw the boat and Fish and Reef and the women with them, she didn't show surprise. She smiled. "Welcome," she said. She waved them on. "Come ashore."

PART TWO

ONE

Darlin woke in the dark. She lay sweating on the mattress she shared with Celia. Leaves and branches scratched the walls and roof of the treehouse like fingernails on a door. In her sleep, Celia had thrown the thin quilt Reef gave them off of herself and piled it onto Darlin. She crawled to the door and then down the ladder, where she sat on the sand and enjoyed feeling the sweat being whisked off her body by the wind. No one was around. She felt like she'd been left alone in someone else's house. She had never been to the island before.

The camp was smaller and shabbier than Reef had described. A large, empty fire ring made of stacked stone crumbled in the center of the site, around which six or eight treehouses sat in the branches of oaks. Most of them looked like they hadn't been inhabited in years, their ladders were missing rungs and their burlap doors hung raggedy. They were painted in faded wild colors, pinks and yellows and blues, but mold and lichen spotted the plywood walls. Moss hung from the roofs. Reef was in one of the rotten treehouses, but she didn't know which. She looked from one to the next, hoping to see the bottoms of his large feet flashing behind the cloth flap, but she didn't.

Only three of the houses looked to have received regular maintenance, and those were the houses that Celia, Fish, and the old woman were, presumably, sleeping in. The walls of those houses were sturdy and new. They were painted robin's egg with red borders. Suns, horses, and tiger stripes muraled their sides. Thin carpet lay over the plank wood floor. The windows were sealed with tight wire screens and, inside, the walls were lined with the colorful spines of books sealed inside of plastic bags to save them from the wet air. Most were mystery novels, but there were also *National Geographic* magazines, recipe books, textbooks, even a high school yearbook. So many books. She had known Reef for three years, but she had never seen him read.

While Celia slept, Darlin had stayed awake. She wanted to know how Reef had been living. There were no framed pictures inside the treehouse. Where she had expected to find a mess, maybe piles of pizza boxes and dirty clothes, she found the place was immaculate. Thin gray cotton sheets covered the mattress. A neat row of empty turtle shells sat atop the bookshelf. A mobile of white driftwood and long brown feathers hung overhead, and from its end dangled a crow's empty skull, staring forever down. She was unsettled by the order of the room.

She had learned early that Reef was tight-lipped about the island. They had agreed to keep their sexual relationship open, and Darlin knew he was sleeping with the old woman, Whistle. She knew he felt connected to her in some way. She was not jealous, but she resented that Reef had kept so much of himself private. His endless evasion. But he said that he loved her. When they were together, they talked about one another. They didn't talk about where they had been and who they had known, they talked about what they were doing and what they wanted to do next, or else they smoked and made love in the tub.

Finally, after two years of hot-and-cold and one year of what Darlin felt was earnest love, they were leaving for Atlanta. She didn't care that the drunken wacko, Derbier, had blown a hole in her door. She didn't care about her grandfather's house, where she lived in secret from most of her family. The future was the only thing that mattered.

She walked some thirty yards until the trees stopped and the beach began. The camp faced the mainland, but it was tucked and hidden away. When Darlin turned on her heels and looked back towards the camp, she saw nothing. Across the sound, the mainland was a dark line on the horizon. She knew Royals was only twenty minutes away, but sitting on the beach with her feet in the cool gray water and the day getting brighter and warmer by degrees, she felt removed from the mainland world and the shouting and gunshots. She felt safe. She listened to the woods groan in the wind and watched a ray patrol the shore.

Something snapped. Darlin turned to see Whistle breaking twigs over a small fire ring at the edge of the woods. The woman had looked like a ghost to Darlin when they arrived in the night, with her wild hair and creepy antique lamp. Now she was hunched over the fire ring, blowing into a pile of tinder with no shirt on and her dugs hanging over the sand. But then a small flame took hold and Whistle fed the fire. When she sat upright, her long silver hair covered her breasts and her blue eyes twinkled under the dark lip of her scar, and she seemed suddenly very beautiful to Darlin, and this filled her with fear.

"Good morning," Whistle said. "Would you like some tea? It'll just take a moment."

"Please," Darlin said.

"How did you sleep?"

"Fine."

They sat and listened to the birds come awake. Darlin worried, briefly, that the old woman was putting her on and might slip a poison berry into her tea to kill her. She didn't know what Whistle knew about her or what she thought. But Whistle fed the fire and soon the water hanging over the flames boiled.

Whistle opened a wooden box near the fire ring and drew out five stained coffee mugs. "Sugar?"

"No thank you."

Whistle closed the box and, carefully, poured water from the pot over small mesh bags. They didn't look like any teabags Darlin had seen before. They had hand-printed labels that read: Dreamwaker. The ink in the words grew blurry and ran as the water was pulled into the teabag's string. Darlin bent to smell the tea.

"It's just peppermint," Whistle said.

"I like the name. I'm Darlin." She wondered if the old woman waded into the water to pee or if she would just have to pick a place in the woods.

Whistle smiled. "Let me show you our outhouse. I should have showed you last night, but I wanted to give you and Celia space."

"How did you know?"

Whistle laughed softly. "It's only natural. Come this way." She led her through the camp, past the steel water pump with its blue chipped head and cedar bucket. Then through a narrow lane of saw palms to what looked to Darlin like the backside of a tall armoire.

The outhouse had no door. The seat of the toilet was made of light, carved wood, and a tin pail of cedar chips and sawdust sat on the floor with a small shovel. The smoky-sweet cedar wafted pleasantly in the breeze as Darlin looked out from the throne.

In front of her, oak limbs bent and contorted in the air over the lush bristle of saw palms. A short sprawl of beach was ornamented with dead behemoth pines. Driftwood towers. They were reverent. Ominous. Like ancient stones. Beyond the trees, the ocean lay like lead.

Darlin unclenched her jaw, and Derbier's swollen, bloody eyes surfaced in her mind. Last night had been a rough end to a long summer. It confirmed the beliefs she held as a child, sent to her grandfather's house in Royals: her belief that Royals was a shrunken, possibly evil place. No one was from Royals. It seemed that people only fell there from some other, higher place. She had slipped up in the city and needed a place to stay, but that was history. An era of her life had gone by sitting on her grandfather's couch and watching TNT. She needed to move.

She considered what she would become to Fish if they moved to Atlanta together. Reef had never talked about bringing Fish before. He only said he was a curious kid that enjoyed island living. Something had changed, recently, for him to want Fish off the island, but he hadn't told her what. In the kitchen, he'd only said that he wouldn't leave the boy behind. For her part, Darlin had come to see Reef's bringing Fish as a mark of his commitment.

She didn't know if Fish would want to leave the island and Whistle. As she watched the tide pool around the driftwood trees from the outhouse, she began to imagine what it would be like to stay on the island.

When she returned to camp, Fish was sitting with Whistle, quickly braiding her hair. Darlin thought the old woman looked like a warrior princess, having her fair hair bound. Her scar curled across her scalp, but it only made her more beautiful. Your eye followed the scar for the pleasure of its curl. She made Darlin's heart race and skin crawl. She could only look at the water when she returned to her tea by the fire ring.

By the time Celia and then, bleary-eyed, Reef came to the cook fire, the sun gleamed through the trees. The furtive trills of the birds inland were outshouted by the contentious sounds of gulls, fighting for the stray legs of crabs.

Fish sat across the fire from Celia. It thrilled him to see her here. Not only because she was pretty and interesting, but because, he thought, she was seeing him at his best and most courageous. She had seen him take down her father. She had seen he could take care of himself and, with the help of his family, that he could take care of her, even Darlin. He sat across from her and smiled, while, silently, he rehashed his fight with Derbier. His slender muscles tensed as he psychically reenacted the drama.

"I want you each to know that you are welcome," Whistle said to Celia and Darlin. "I'm sorry for the manner that you've come to this island, but I'm glad you are here."

"Thank you," the women said.

"Our friend Nutzo is missing and may be hurt. I'll be searching for him today, but you are welcome to the treehouse and what food we have. Reef will show you where we hang the larder."

"Whistle," Reef said. He had set down the orange he was peeling. "Where could you have gone that we didn't go?"

"The southern marshes," she said.

The entire southern tip of the island was marsh. It made a great cushion against the driving storm waters, but it was a maze of shifting rivers and thick, soft mud. It was difficult for Fish to imagine Nutzo, able as he was, going into the marshes on foot. Every step would sink to the knee at least. As far as Fish knew, there was no shelter there, no dry land or trees, save a few driftwood specters.

"You think he had some sort of break? You can't stay out there."

"I was there last night, and it's no different than any other marsh. Just not many places to stand. I used the canoe."

Reef put his head in his hands. "What have you found?"

"There's a lot more ground to cover, so I won't have time to stay around camp today," Whistle said. "And I understand that you think he left the island. Maybe you think I'm in denial and fabricating this all. I understand. But I am telling you that while I slept last night, I dreamt that Nutzo was sleeping beside me and that we were in the southern marshes."

"You really dreamed that?" Darlin asked.

"Yes, I did."

"Darlin," Reef said.

"What? I didn't say I don't believe her. I'm just curious is all."

"There's no need to explain yourself, Darlin," Whistle said. "Do you remember your dreams?"

"Yeah," Darlin said. She looked to Celia and smirked. "Sometimes I write the good ones down."

"It's real interesting stuff," Celia said.

"And do you believe your dreams translate useful information to you, taken from your subconscious mind? Taken from the things you see, the tiniest of details, and that these things add up to what some people call a 'gut' impulse?" Whistle asked.

"I do."

"Then you'll know why I have to keep looking for my friend,

and you," she turned to Reef, "know more than you're letting on. I know I have been delicate when discussing Sugar—" she paused. "I've been prickly when discussing the tiger in the past, but it is now clear to me that he is no longer suited to live with us here. He's a danger, and I will arrange for him to leave." Tears filled her eyes. "I'm so sorry, Fish."

"It's okay," Fish said. He didn't fight to keep his lip from quivering. He was glad she was taking up for him and talking about getting rid of Sugar, but he was also beginning to consider that he didn't need Whistle to do for him. He could do for himself. And she hadn't done anything yet.

Feeling full with his new powers of violence, he had forgotten the tiger existed. It seemed like his future was swinging on a chain, and that it was coming around again, back from Atlanta and the smell of tar and towards the island, racing like a ball of hot steel. He didn't believe in angels, but there had been signs that he was about to come into vast capability. He had been attacked, and he had lived. He won the fight with Derbier. He had the handheld. Celia was here. Whatever he willed, the universe provided. His head swam with the implications.

Maybe he had earned this, he thought. By fighting off Sugar, twice, maybe he had proven to someone or something that he had heavy sand, and that he was here to be somebody who won fights and ran away to islands with beautiful women. He had manifested this.

"It would change everything to have him gone," Fish said. He reached to hold Whistle's hand.

"Thank you," she said. "Reef, you know Nutzo kept caches. We don't know where they all are. If he's out there. If he's hurt at one of those caches." She held up her hands. "He could have enough supplies to last for a week or more."

"I checked all the caches that I know," Reef said.

"You should look for him," Darlin said. "We can spare the days. Celia, have you thought about what you want to do?"

Celia shook her head no. She had been quiet through the morning, content to sip her tea and listen. "If my dad is in jail, he'll have told the police that I'm living with him in Royals. He might send them here."

"Do you have somewhere else to be?" Whistle asked.

"My mom's place in Savannah."

"Is that where you want to be?"

"You don't care that the police might come here?"

"I'm not worried about that for now. What do you want to do?"

Her mother, Berny, was in Florida with her newest boyfriend. Released from Derbier, she had flourished and, she told Celia, rediscovered herself in her middle years. She had been a marathon runner but tore her knee badly. In the three months she was confined to the house, reliant almost entirely on Derbier, problems that had lived, quietly, under the surface of their marriage became unavoidable. They were divorced the summer before Celia entered the sixth grade. Derbier kept the assets related to his charter fishing business and Celia's mother kept their large Savannah home.

Celia loved her mother, but they weren't close. She thought of Berny as Berny. She imagined her, always, in the glimmering blue dress she once sent Celia a picture of herself wearing. She would be smoking a long cigarette and pretending to be a Parisian sophisticate like her heroes in the movies. From Berny, Celia consciously took her love of life, and the tenacious belief she carried that, No, it needn't be that way, and Yes, it could be her way after all.

For the last week, her boyfriend, Adam, had been hounding her to come back to Savannah where they had the run of Berny's empty house, skipping school and part-time jobs to lounge in Berny's hot tub in their underwear. They had been dating for six months, and Adam had begun to ask for sex. It was, he said, really cool, and besides, he knew Celia had had sex with the last guy she dated, Paul Francen. Paul had told him. They had been arguing about it when Celia's arm was broken.

The only thing that kept Adam from driving to Royals and "stealing her back" was that his brother's car was on two donuts and couldn't risk the trip. He had pitched the idea that Celia use Berny's card to buy new tires, but that, she said, was too much. Berny would notice and blow the whole thing up, even though Berny wouldn't notice, and likely wouldn't confront Celia if she did.

Since Adam had slammed her arm in the doorway of Berny's Savannah house, Berny had been extra generous, and Celia had been dodging Adam. When Berny heard of what Celia called a freak accident, she suggested Celia stay with Derbier, as she was often forced to do in the summer. Besides Darlin, there was nothing in Royals for Celia besides space from Adam, but she had agreed to go and called Derbier, who seemed grateful and dumbfounded to pick her up.

"You know it was an accident, right?" Adam asked her when she told him she would have to go to Royals. She'd had to promise him that she did know that, but it wasn't the first time he had pushed her or snatched at her arm or clothes when they argued. He'd gotten comfortable with her, she thought. Now he wasn't afraid to reach for what he wanted. She had seen it happen to Paul Francen.

"I'd like to stay here for a while longer. As long as Darlin stays."

Whistle nodded. "You're welcome to stay under the condition that you tell your mother you're here camping with friends. I will take you to the marina and we'll learn more there. The sheriff will have already called your people."

"I'll do that," Celia said.

They decided that Whistle and Celia would go that morning to the marina, and that Reef, Darlin, and Fish would search for Nutzo's caches in the southern marsh. They wouldn't meet again until the evening.

Fish was discussing possible cache locations of Nutzo's with Reef when Celia called him to where she had gathered with her things by the cook fire. She was waiting on Whistle.

"Thank you for your help last night," she said.

"You're welcome," Fish said. "I'm glad you're staying."

"Only if my mom doesn't freak out, but she's pretty laid back."

"It's just cool that you wanted to be here," Fish said.

"You think so?" Celia liked Fish. He didn't run his mouth in a way that displeased her. Maybe he was too young, she thought, but he had cool hair, he could draw, and he seemed to have ideas. "I'll see you tonight," she said. "If I don't come back, you can send your letters to Darlin."

She wanted to see the horses. She wanted to be away from Adam and Derbier. She wished, for Berny's sake, that a small camera would appear and film her, in black and white, knocking the ash from a long cigarette while Fish grinned stupidly at her on a white sand beach.

TWO

Reef found the omen in the sand a few minutes from camp. He didn't touch the bird, only called Fish to see where it lay sprawled in the middle of the game trail. It looked like it had been dead a decade. It was flattened. Its eyes had dried and disappeared.

A year ago, Reef woke to find a dead gull hanging from a tree in camp, swinging in the wind. It had eaten a hook and tangled itself in the branches with the fishing line. He cut it down and, the same day, fell through a roof in Royals while laying shingling and impaled his foot on a nail. When Whistle drove him to get a tetanus shot, the truck blew a tire and nearly killed them. They had walked home, too afraid to hitch a ride. Whistle burned sage.

Fish poked at the body with a stick. It was light, like a mat of reeds. "It must have died months ago," he said. He studied the tops of the trees nearby. Oaks and a few palms. The pelican must have been blown from one of them. He imagined it tumbling like a leaf, its wings half-extended and its neck permanently bent. It seemed important to know where the bird came from.

"Birds die," Darlin said. "Let's keep going." The legs of her jeans swished down the game trail. She picked up a snapped limb for a walking stick. She bobbed her head, dramatically, to avoid a spider's web. "This island is beautiful."

Reef frowned at Fish and followed Darlin along the path. The sky was cloudless and the foliage bright, but he was chilled. The sun made his skin itch. When he was confined to the stale, wet kitchen of his cousin's restaurant in Atlanta, he would miss the nights he lay cool and dry on the dunes. But that was his play. If he wanted to get Fish off of the island, it was kitchen work or trying to make it on his own. He had hoped they could stay at Darlin's.

He had spent a summer of afternoons replacing fixtures and carpet in Darlin's aging house. He had built the small bathing porch from the ground, and he had conceived a plan to marry Darlin and legally adopt Fish, then get a job with the army and escape them. But even if Darlin had approved of Fish moving in—and she had been on the fence—her uncle was selling the house. Cashing in on all of Reef's work. So the dream of another summer in the claw-foot tub dried up. Now Darlin had to figure something out too. So he would wash dishes for a little while with his cousin. He had done it before. He didn't worry about Whistle. They had been apart before. Love moved freely between them.

The tiger was why they had to leave now, but it wasn't all of why he wanted to leave. He saw his leaving as a natural progression into the next adventure. He knew Whistle would understand, because he remembered the afternoons in Atlanta, the hours he spent lying on her office floor while she drew out what he wanted most. They had worked together at the rehab, he as a treatment advocate, driving and fetching patients, and she as a therapist. He knew she was married when he approached her at work, but it was fine, she said. Her husband knew she was polyamorous. They began meeting after her morning group.

"It's only natural that you should want to leave," she said. She loved to lay her face in his spread hand while she lay against his leg. Her jaw hummed under his thumb. "You can't find what you want in the city."

"What do I want?"

"You want to come with me to the island."

"I don't want to go camping for a year."

"You want to be comfortable, but you don't want to waste away. You want to use your body. You want to be in desperate situation, and you want to win."

He was, at that time, at his most extreme in his workout regimen and weighed two-hundred and six pounds. It was a number he thought of often. Before his dreadlocks, Reef kept his head shaved and enjoyed watching the muscles define themselves against his scalp when he chewed. "I'm not wasting away."

"Spiritually." She sat up to face him. "You must feel predictable?"

The rehab clinic was Reef's second job. He drove the patients there until two, then worked nights with his cousin. In between that, he did landscaping work for his uncle on the weekends. He shared an apartment with two of the most degenerate men to graduate from his high school and the three of them stayed in the bars all through Little Five-Points. He was, at that time, in active sexual relationships with eleven people, all polyamorous women in middle age. He'd met them all through Whistle.

"I don't feel predictable at all."

Whistle had smiled. "I'm glad," she said. She never spoke to Reef about the island again. The men and women Reef saw through Whistle's network of lovers spoke of it endlessly over the next few weeks. Whistle had it worked out with the people there, they said. No bills and a paying job on the beach.

"You would be the youngest in the colony," the women told him.

"We could really use you."

"What's keeping you here?"

Reef distanced himself. He stopped seeing Whistle and quit the job at the clinic, which had largely sucked. Months passed and he immersed himself in his routine, which defined itself as having sex with his one girlfriend, getting into fights with his cousin over money, and working at the restaurant, which cut his gym time.

He felt he had been courted by a cult and had narrowly escaped, except no one was interested in congratulating him. He had freed himself to the monotony of safety. To Reef, it felt like something had passed him by. A brush with a life that would be, he knew, a reflection of Whistle's whim, but it was wild. He waited to feel proud for making progress towards an assistant manager spot at the restaurant, but found himself feeling sure that he had slunk away from the maximum expression of the independence that was possible to him. He had to have it. He started seeing Whistle again.

But Bomb Island had become a death trap, and he was tired of living as Whistle's second. He had been her right hand. Now she had put herself into a difficult situation and what she needed was to swallow her pride and to follow him to Atlanta. That was the next chapter, and she would have the same choice he had, to stay or go. After ten years on the island, Reef's dreams had stretched far away, and he would follow.

They tunneled north through the forest, side-stepping the tight brown turds of the horses that maintained the trail with their endless patrolling. From time to time, two brown mares appeared behind them to stare, either curious or paranoid.

As they neared the marsh, the sand began to thicken and sprout. They found Nutzo's gondola where the dry land ended, and they poled it through the few serpentine creeks that were wide enough for them to pass through. They took turns coaxing and shoving the clunky vessel with the bamboo poles.

It was absurd, Reef thought, to look for Nutzo with his own boat. How would he have gotten to any of the caches they managed to find? Because Whistle had a dream. But he was here, doing it. He expected to find nothing and hoped, at least, Darlin was enjoying herself. She was sitting on the raft and dangling her feet in the brown water, staring into the marsh with deadly seriousness.

"There," she said. A red spot of paint marked a tree that stuck from the mud. It was Nutzo's mark, but when they tied the raft to the bank and looked around the base of the tree, they didn't see anything. The breeze died, and the mosquitos bombarded them.

"He wouldn't make it that easy," Fish said.

"Who was he trying to fool?" Darlin asked. "No one out here."

"He's careful is all."

Reef stood on the raft, looking at the tree with the spot. This is where Nutzo would have stood, he thought. He didn't know for sure, but it had probably been years ago. The old man had made it a regular practice to walk the island, end to end. He slept away from camp for weeks at a time and maintained his caches regularly. Reef and the others had made a game of Nutzo's familiarity with the island by leaving him messages in the knots and holes of odd-shaped trees. He never failed to leave a reply.

Under a thornbush, they found one of the gray plastic bins that Nutzo stored his caches in. Inside of the bin was a plastic grocery bag of pecans, a can of SPAM, and two gallons of water. All of it was marked with the pink price stickers used by the marina store. There was no sign that Nutzo had been here recently.

They moved on, pushing the raft through the small salt rivers into the afternoon. The sun grew unbearable. They put the poles down and drifted, huddled in the shade of the raft's blue tarp awning and cracking the pecans, two-a-hand. When the raft beached itself on a low mudbank, a heron flew down to stalk around its edges where minnows hid in the shade.

"Do you really think he's in Atlanta?" Fish asked quietly.

"He could be anywhere," Reef said. "He kept to himself."

"So he could be here?"

"Maybe," Reef said. "What do you think? You heard what she's dreaming." He was watching the tops of the marsh grass grow shorter in the rising tide and thinking that there couldn't be any caches this far into the marsh where they would be washed over twice a day. Still, it had felt good to find the pecan cache with its hand-scrawled inventory, dated three years ago. It felt like saying goodbye.

He had never been attracted to Nutzo, but the nights they lay with Whistle together, he felt reassured by his presence. He reveled in the security and freedom of their treehouse, where they had discovered a comfort that would have been impossible anywhere else. He figured the old man had finally decided to walk into the forest and disappear. More than any of them, even Whistle, he believed in the restoration that came from spending long periods of time in the woods.

"I hope he's not out here," Fish said.

"Exactly."

"So what are we doing?"

Reef tossed a pecan shell at Fish. "We're looking for Nutzo, and we're laying low until we can get Darlin's things from the house and go to Atlanta. I think we could go tonight. It's not safe here."

"I'm not afraid of Sugar," Fish said.

"Well you should be."

"Well I'm not."

"Well you're not going to last long like that."

"You trying to scare me off this island?" Fish shouted. His voice scattered out over the vastness of the marsh and was absorbed. The heron flew away.

"I'm trying to do what's best," Reef said calmly. "She can't control him. He's a time bomb."

"Sugar never hurts Whistle, and when I stood up to him the other night, he left me alone too. When Derbier was coming for Celia and me, we put him down. They can tell when you're afraid. That's the secret."

"The secret?" Reef put his hands over his eyes and rubbed the sockets hard. His muscles tensed. "Will you listen to me? The tiger is going to kill you."

If they left for Atlanta tonight, he might never see Celia again.

"You're scared," Fish said. "Because of the omen."

Reef threw a nut into the deck of the raft, and it sounded like a gunshot. "Fucking child."

He stood and took up his pole and shoved the raft into the river, only now they were headed back the way they had come. "The tide is too high to find anything here." No one argued.

The marsh was filling up. Creeks that had been a foot deep and yellow were swollen and dark. New ways through the marsh opened, and Reef pushed the raft in a meandering path towards dry land, grunting with exertion. A light, misting rain came upon them in broad day.

"Why do they call him that?" Darlin asked. "Nutzo. It doesn't seem like something you would want to be called."

"He dug it," Reef said. "He earned it too, crazy dude."

Fish sat in silence. He didn't know what Reef would tell her. It was against the rules to tell a name story to someone who didn't live on the island. No one had told Fish that these were the rules, but he had never seen them broken. Whenever a tourist overhead John-Elvis talking to Whistle at the dock, and asked her, sometimes they tugged on her sleeve to ask, "Is that your real name?" Whistle only smiled. "I'm Dutch," she would say to the tourist. "Hey, Dutch," Fish always replied.

"It was from something in Atlanta," Reef began.

"Dude," Fish said.

"That's not a real rule," Reef said, but after finding the omen, and with the day-rain on, he stopped.

"These are secret names?" Darlin asked Fish. "You said you used to be a surfer," she said to Reef.

"I was," he said.

"It's tradition," Fish said. "I'm sorry."

"You think Darlin is my real name?"

He had thought it was her name. It had never occurred to him that people on Royals might have found names. Whistle said it was an old tradition to wait for your name to come. When he told this to Jonathan, the older boy had laughed. "Those are just nicknames," he said, but they were more than that. They were powerful to Fish.

He loved to walk through the marina and feel he carried a mystery with him. No one knew why he was called Fish and not Robert. He considered his Fish parts his best. They were the parts he had discovered himself or that had been shown to him by powerful forces, Whistle and Sugar and even the bomb. They were all part of Fish's story, whereas Robert's story ended in an apartment fire in Atlanta. If they gave Nutzo's story to Darlin, it would dilute the story. It would become hers to tell.

"My name was Susa," Darlin said. She was sitting, cross-legged under the tarp. Dark marsh mud streaked her arms, and the rain made her hair huge.

"It was where my grandfather met his wife. He was a soldier for the English, and his convoy broke down outside of the ruins. Susa used to be a very large city. In the war, it became a place used by bandits. My grandfather's convoy was attacked. He was the only one to survive."

"Is that real?" Fish asked. He had forgotten that he was angry with Reef.

"I don't know. It was told to me like it was real."

"Why don't you like it?"

"I like it fine."

"Then why don't you use it?"

"I like Darlin better."

"Why Darlin?" Fish asked.

She only raised her eyebrow at him.

Fish considered that she had spent the night at the island already and that Reef would probably tell her anyway. With Nutzo maybe gone, not many people knew the story. He didn't want to let it go. But he had liked her Susa story. He didn't know why he had been named Robert. He wondered if it was part of a war story or if he was meant to have a normal, peacetime name.

"You can tell her," he said to Reef. "She's with us."

Darlin smiled.

"I will never forget this shit," Reef said. "It was in Atlanta. Kyle and I were supposed to meet Whistle's ex-husband, a wacko. Guy's clothes were too tight or something. He always looked like he was going to pop. He was an assistant principal somewhere. Anyway, he had been separated from Whistle for a long time, but he had a bunch of her stuff, like books and shit. And he was finally going to give it back to her, but she figured it was just a play to get to her—this is the guy who eventually shot her—anyway, so she sent me and—" Reef laughed. "Me and Kyle out to go meet the guy and get her books. It was summer and hot as shit, but we were rolling in this sweet Jeep that was Kyle's brother's. One of those big rock climbing ones. We had all the doors off and we cruised up to the Hardee's where we were supposed to meet the guy, and there's a high school band there."

"What?" Darlin asked.

"It was like twenty kids in the Hardee's parking lot," Reef said.

"Thirty," Fish said.

"Tubas, trombones. The guy was out there with flowers in his too-tight work clothes and had paid or, like, made these kids play 'Sweet Caroline.' I guess he thought Whistle was coming. When we told him we were there for her stuff, he immediately lost it. He threw his clipboard at the Jeep!" Reef slapped his chest. "He was like, 'Fuck you! Blah! Fucking pawns!'"

"With the kids there?"

"Oh, the kids were freaked the fuck out! They were just watching this shit. We tried to talk to him. Like 'Easy, dude. We're just here for the books.' He seemed pretty harmless. And he was like, 'I'll take them to her myself,' and started shouting the address of the place we were staying at. He just kept shouting it."

"Shit."

"And then Kyle, for the last time on this earth, Kyle drove that tall, badass Jeep towards this dude, and the guy jumps out of the way, and Nutzo drove over this guy's car. It was one of those long silver towncars. He monster-trucked it. The tries blew out. We crushed the roof, the windshield, everything."

"Alright."

"No, that's not even it. Nutzo then gets out of the Jeep. The kids are scattered. The Hardee's guys are coming out of the store, like, waving and shouting and shit. Nutzo pulls open the crushed-ass door of this guy's car and gets Whistle's little box of books from the back seat, and when the guy comes at him, he just gives this like, wild scream, right in the dude's face, and the guy fell down on the ground. It literally floored him. We just drove off."

Fish laughed. He had never seen a new person hear this story before. He had only heard it aloud once, from Nutzo himself, who presented the story simply as "I ran over a guy's car" when Fish asked. He was glad Darlin could hear it this way and that this would be the story that survived Nutzo, if he were actually dead.

"So what happened?" Darlin asked. "They had to have called the cops."

"Yeah," Reef said. "We had to ditch the Jeep. Nutz's brother took it to Dahlonega. But we never had any trouble from police. The guy had his own problems and wasn't going to call the cops."

"And then he shot her?"

"That was later," Reef said.

"How much later?"

"About a month."

"There!" Fish said. He pointed from the raft to a red piece of cloth that stuck above the marsh grass. It looked like it was attached to a piece of metal.

When they approached, they found the cloth was part of a sun-roof. A whole boat lay cast up in the marsh grass. It looked to have been thrown there in a storm, but it must have been years ago. A small, stunted tree grew next to the boat. The small patch of earth might have remained hidden forever by the tall marsh grass that hemmed it in from all sides. The seats and fixtures had been destroyed by the sun and rain.

Reef hauled Nutzo's gray cache box from the back of the boat. Inside were two gallons of water and three bags of pecans. The inventory note was from the same date as the last cache, and listed the supplies except it also listed Civ.Or. X 12. Reef didn't know what that meant. He studied Nutzo's scribble. The inventory said there should be twelve of the Civ. Or., but the gray bin was empty besides the water and nuts.

"Check the cabin," Reef told Fish.

In the crawl space set into the boat's hull, the air stank with rot. Fish covered his nose with his arm. There was nothing there, only rags. In the corner lay a strangled knot of plastic mesh that might once have been net. It was a small fishing boat, apparently abandoned. The key jutted from the ignition, comically. The plastic steering wheel was broken off.

"If he had taken them himself, whatever they are, he would have marked it."

"Reef," Darlin said. She pulled a small, blue cooler from the tall grass. It had been tied with twine to a stake in the ground. "It's heavy." She set the cooler on the ground by the boat, and they gathered around it.

When Darlin opened the lid she saw that it was lined with clear glass Coke bottles, each filled with powder and steel shot and capped. Fuses fed into the bottles and were wrapped in plastic to keep dry. "Shit," she said. She backed away from the cooler.

"Fucking hell," Reef said. It was homemade dynamite, used for fishing. Twelve charges of it. They were on Nutzo's list so he obviously knew they were here. He must have found them in the boat when he made the cache. Reef had never known Nutzo to cache weapons before. He had been in the army, but he never spoke of it. The old man didn't hunt and would never blast fish. "We should destroy it," he said. "It's bad shit."

"I think we should just walk away and leave it the hell alone," Darlin said. "The rain will destroy it in an hour. I know some people who used to do this. It's messed up and not safe, especially when the stuff gets old."

"I'll just pour some water on it," Reef said. He reached for the gallon Nutzo had stashed.

"Stop!" Darlin said. "I'm serious. It could go off."

Reef set the water down. "Alright. Okay."

Fish was still staring at the Coke bottle bombs. He was trying to take them apart with his eyes.

"Let's do it Darlin's way," Reef said. "Come on, and let's get back. Nutz hasn't been here in years."

While Reef and Darlin fought the marsh to get back to the raft, Fish slid the lid of the cooler closed and lifted it inside the hull of the boat, and as he did, he conjured a plan to keep his family together on Bomb Island. In his time living on the island he had learned from wise and terrible masters. He knew that pelicans did not fall dead in the path for no reason. He believed he was in love and that the world was beginning to open to him. He believed in the priestess, Whistle, because her dream had led him to this tool.

THREE

Celia's mother didn't answer when she called from the phone that hung from the wall in the marina store. It didn't surprise Celia, who knew Berny was traveling with her beau. It didn't seem like anyone was looking for her in Royals. No police were at the docks. No dogs patrolled the boat trailers lined in their fields of grass. While Whistle talked with the old marina man, John-Elvis, in a back room of the dusty store, Celia ate a pack of peanut butter crackers at a gray folding table and prepared to fake the conversation she couldn't have with Berny.

It had been a cool, gentle morning, and the sound had been flat. Light filled the store and its shelves of supplies and souvenirs. Most of the coffee mugs, shirts, and hats were bright pink and had cartoon images of the bomb printed on them. Outside, the machines that pumped oxygen into the large livewell of bait fish and shrimp droned. Men lowered a white boat into the water with a droning electric hoist and clinking chains. Celia dialed her mother's number again. She pressed her finger on the receiver to end the call when Berny's answering machine began to speak.

"Mom," she said into the dead phone. Loud enough that she was sure Whistle could hear. "I guess you heard, Dad got into a fight." She paused. "I'm fine and camping with friends."

"Thank goodness you weren't hurt. Who knows what he might have done?" the voice of Imaginary Berny said. "You didn't know the party was going to get that out of hand."

"It was under control."

"You did so well, shooting that mace into your father's eyes. And then that boy kicked him in the throat! I bet it hurts for him to breathe."

"Yeah. We're lucky no one was hurt."

"I'm so proud of you, Cee-Cee. You're the image of a strong, adventurous young woman. What's that? Where am I? I'm probably on a boat in Southern Europe or some shit."

"No, don't feel like you have to rush back. I'm fine here. I'm staying with Darlin."

"Don't worry, baby. I won't rush. You probably won't see me until Christmas. We haven't talked since your boyfriend broke your arm, and when you asked me to come home, I asked, 'How bad is it?' Well, how bad is it now?"

"It's good. We're sleeping in treehouses. We made tea over a fire."

"How are you planning on breaking up with Adam, Cee-Cee? You didn't call him last night or this morning, and you don't want to call him now. Doesn't he have a key to my house anyway? What about your dad? They won't keep him away forever. Who will you call to get you back to Savannah? He knows all your friends."

Celia began to cry. She hung up the phone and sat at a table covered in used newspapers and empty coffee cups. "Goodbye. I love you," she said, but the imaginary mother she had called was still talking to her.

"You can't go back to your dad's. I guess you'll have to call Adam to get you. He'll drive down for sure when he hears about this. A party like that, he probably has heard. Weren't some of those kids from the Benedict school?"

Celia wiped her nose on her shirt. She felt worn down. Her arm ached in its cast. She swore she could feel the broken ends of the bone where they smashed against one another, not yet fused. She walked back to the phone and dialed Adam's house.

"You'll probably have to sleep with him," Imaginary Berny said. "You can't ask him to drive all this way and then break up with him. What would he do then? Be careful, Cee-Cee."

Adam answered on the first ring. "Babe?"

"Hey."

"That's all you've got to say after two days of nothing? Are you crying?"

"Ask him to come get you!" Imaginary Berny hissed. "You really like this guy. He's sweet! He loves you!"

"My mom's coming back tonight," Celia said.

"Oh shit. So you're coming back?"

"What are you doing? He loves you," Berny said. "He didn't mean to hurt you. Accidents happen. Don't be so sensitive."

Celia dried her face with her shirttail. She took a deep breath, held it in her chest, then exhaled slowly. It helped.

"You're coming back, babe," Adam said.

"I'm going to meet her, but we're leaving tonight for Bermuda."

"What?" Adam's voice broke. "You can't do that."

"It's out of my hands."

"How long will you be gone?"

"I don't know. Maybe just the rest of summer. But if things go well with Mom and this new guy, maybe longer. They have international school there."

"Is this about your arm? Jesus, is it over that?"

"It's not about that," Celia said. "It's not that at all. It just is what it is."

"Oh my God. I won't let her do this. That bitch. Your asshole dad. He's why you're leaving. I should have come and gotten you sooner."

"Don't worry," Celia said. "I'm leaving for the airport now. I'm meeting my mom in Miami. That's where we'll fly from."

"Oh God. I'll be there. When is the flight? I won't let them take you, babe. I'll fight for you. Will you fight for us?"

"Don't go to Miami. I don't know where we're leaving from. The guy is really wealthy. It's a private airfield."

"If this is about your arm. It was an accident. It was not my fault. And you know you set me off when you said that thing. You know I don't do well when you talk about that stuff."

"I have to go. Goodbye."

"Celia, don't you hang up this fucking phone. Ce—"

Celia hung up the phone. She sat back down at the table and rested her head on its cool, pleather top. She closed her eyes. With her mother undisturbed on her travels, Derbier detained by the police for now, and Adam not expecting her in Savannah or Royals, she felt pleasantly alone. She was surrounded by strangers that didn't know anything about her, except what they could see and what she told them. She imagined this was how her mother felt when she traveled to exotic places with men she barely knew. It was empowering. It felt safe.

"Are you ready to go?" Whistle asked.

Celia jerked her face from the tabletop. "Almost." A piece of plastic from the cracker wrapper was stuck to her cheek, and she pulled it off. She guessed Whistle had heard her conversation with Adam, but she wasn't asking her about it.

John-Elvis appeared in the doorway behind Whistle. "Let's go and get it then," he said.

"Will you come with us?" Whistle asked. "Or I can meet you at the dock in fifteen minutes, if your mother agrees with you staying with us."

"Why are you letting me stay?"

"It's not my island," Whistle said. "Mr. John-Elvis's family owns a large portion of the land, and the rest is owned by the state. He has agreed to let you stay."

"So longs you stay with Darlin," John-Elvis said. He was a thin, bald man with white stubble covering his wobbly jowls. He wore a white t-shirt tucked into his ancient blue jeans. His accent was severe.

"Thank you," Celia said.

"An you don't have to worry about your daddy."

"I don't worry, sir."

John-Elvis scratched his face. "Alright," he grumbled. He leaned behind the register's counter and pulled a small can of mace and handed it to Celia. "Nice to meet you, miss."

"Nice to meet you," Celia said. She put the mace in her backpack. "I'll see you at the dock, Whistle. Fifteen minutes."

"Very well," Whistle said, and she and John-Elvis walked from the store.

Celia watched them cross the road to one of the marina's large storage buildings—places where boats were boarded for months at a time. John-Elvis cracked the bay door for Whistle, and the two of them disappeared inside. She knew she didn't have much time.

When she grabbed her bag after the party, she'd only thrown a few things inside. A pair of jeans, a handful of shirts, a wad of underwear and socks. She didn't know where she would have to stay or for how long.

She jogged to Derbier's house. Except for her father's garish orange truck parked sideways in the front yard, the house looked fine from the outside. A few cups poked from the bushes. She walked around the house, and the dew wet her toes. The front and back doors were locked.

In the driveway she found a marvel: a model of an Egyptian pyramid made from silver beer cans. At its base, it was two feet long on all sides. She felt a pressing urge to kick the pyramid, but didn't. Somehow, it had survived the fallout of the party. It didn't seem right to destroy it now. May it last a thousand years.

She pulled at the door handles of Derbier's truck, and they didn't give. She could see her father's keys still in the truck's ignition. She needed to get inside. The small, square window over the truck's bed was cracked, and she slid it back. Even with the window at its widest, it would be a squeeze. Celia held her arms over her head and stepped through the window onto Derbier's back seat. Her cast knocked against the glass, and she had to contort her body to adjust for her arm's frozen L-bend, but she was in. She took the keys from the ignition and unlocked the center console of the truck, where Derbier kept the key to his boat. She stuffed it in her bag and used Derbier's keys to unlock the front door of the house.

Inside, empty plastic cups lay beside wet clothing, cigarette butts, and broken glass. The punch cooler had been flipped and sticky red film covered the kitchen floor. Celia rushed to repack her backpack with sturdier clothes and her father's rain poncho. She put on her hiking boots and left the leather-strap sandals she'd been wearing on the floor. Next, she searched Derbier's bedroom.

The master looked empty without its large bed, and the furniture was either destroyed or had survived being thrown against the wall by making large holes in the drywall. There was a pile of broken picture frames in the corner, and she kicked through them to see images of a much younger Derbier with Berny. There were pictures of Celia too. Most of them taken when she was a baby.

She had decided to throw the party after Derbier refused to take her back to Savannah, thinking to force his hand. When he had been married to Berny, Derbier had insisted on driving her to work and picking her up. He had been obsessed with controlling her movements. When Berny ran her marathons, Derbier would wait with Celia at the finish line, ready to throw Berny in the passenger seat and whisk her home. Berny cried each time she completed a race.

"It's just runner's nerves," she had said.

Even at his worst, Derbier never threatened them with a gun. She thought of the way his face was twisted and red when he burst through the back door of the house and came for her and Fish. It had been unrecognizable.

In the weeks she had been here, Derbier had been distant, focused on his business and what he called his "neighborhood watch," which consisted of spying on people around town with a night vision camera, including Whistle and the hippies of Bomb Island. Derbier had never spoken to Celia about the project. She had only seen the pictures.

Celia found her father's dented nightstand in the back of the closet where it had been hurled like a cannonball. She had to struggle against a pile of Derbier's clothes to turn the thing over. Someone had upended a bottle of shoe polish on the floor and used it to draw peace signs and smiley faces. In the top drawer of the nightstand was a large yellow envelope, which Celia slid into her pack. She stuck her hand in the drawer and felt around for more, but there was nothing.

She checked the middle and bottom drawers and found them filled with shotgun shells, packets of peanuts, and tax documents. She knew that this was where Derbier kept his important things, so where were his spare keys? She looked through the debris on the floor of the bedroom, but the keys weren't there. She knew that Whistle would be leaving soon. She checked the toolbox of the truck, but they weren't there either.

Celia ran to marina. From the shore, she saw Whistle and John-Elvis hugging on the dock near the glass-bottom boat. Then the marina man gave Whistle his hand as she stepped, like a queen, into the boat. Celia had never known her grandmothers, and the old woman fascinated her. She liked the way Whistle asked her what she wanted. She wondered what Whistle thought of the lie she had told Adam, and, Celia was surprised to discover, she wanted Whistle to like her.

"Hey! Wait!" Celia called down.

Whistle waved her on from the boat. She was smiling. "That didn't take long," she said when Celia was aboard. "Would you like to see the bomb on our way back?"

"Yes."

At the site, Whistle dropped the anchor off the bow. "I'm sorry, you won't be able to swim down," she said. She nodded to the green cast on Celia's arm.

"This is alright," Celia said. "I've never seen it before."

She was sitting on the bench seat and leaning over the glass bottom, staring at the gray blur that was the bomb. She thought of her father's railing at the stupidity of allowing people to tour, what he said, was a live weapon, but, more often, he complained of the monopoly Whistle and John-Elvis had on the tours.

The old woman slipped off her thong sandals and drew off her white sun cover to reveal a black one-piece swimsuit. Celia had seen her swimming naked this morning and rubbing her body with fine gray sand that she scooped from the bottom. Whistle's muscles pulled and threshed like thin steel cables beneath her sun-spotted skin.

The bomb looked small and sleepy from the boat. An undersea wind kicked up sand, and the steel shell disappeared altogether. Celia didn't see what the big deal was. "You're going in?" she asked.

"Yes, while the water is calm."

"You aren't scared the police will come get you?"

"Why would they come get me?"

"For, like, having a tiger. If they knew, they would come, right?"

Whistle sat down on the bench seat. "Celia, you don't need to worry about that. It's impossible to keep a tiger secret forever, and soon Sugar will be off the island. I've seen to it."

Celia opened her backpack and pulled out Derbier's yellow envelope. "I need to show you this."

Inside the envelope were green-and-gray-tinted photographs of Sugar and Whistle. In most of the photos, the tiger was crouched in the dunes or lying on the beach, and Whistle meditated on her reed mat. They were together in one of the pictures. Whistle's white head was looking at Sugar, who seemed to be jumping in the air. It was the clearest of the batch.

"He was catching shells," Whistle said.

"What?"

"Sugar, in that picture. I was throwing shells to him, in the dark, and he was catching them in his paws."

"Derbier took these," Celia said. "My dad."

"I know, dear. I've seen him around. If he could have done anything with those"—she pointed to the pictures—"he would have done it."

"I guess."

Whistle opened the small gate-door in the stern and climbed down a small ladder to get in the water. "I know it," she said, and slid beneath the water.

Celia watched the old woman swim. She moved so naturally that she seemed to slide rather than push her way to the bottom. She waved up at Celia, and Celia waved back. Who was this lady?

With Whistle's body providing a sense of scale, the bomb seemed to double in size. It was nearly as long as the boat. Maybe longer. Celia leaned down and pressed her face to the glass bottom, but she couldn't see much better. There were no symbols painted on the bomb. It looked to Celia like an enormous manatee buried in the sand. A killer manatee.

"How many times have you swum with it?" she asked Whistle after the old woman had climbed back onto the deck and dried herself with a towel.

"Many," she said. "Hundreds, at least. When I was young, we buried pennies around it for good luck."

"You don't worry about it?"

"No."

"Because of your religion."

Whistle laughed. "No, because I believe what the Navy divers believed—that it was a dummy core. It's had plenty of opportunities to explode since it was dropped. A hurricane all but threw it fifty yards. But I do think it provides a valuable lesson."

"Disarmament?"

"That we are drawn to symbols of power. That being near power reveals us. The bomb exposes what we want."

"I guess you have to swim with it to understand," Celia said. She didn't want to be rude, but it was a dead bomb. It hadn't revealed anything to her, but she believed Whistle was a woman who always had a plan. She wouldn't dismiss the bomb, for Whistle's sake. She assumed the old woman used her comfort with the bomb to build a reputation and a business.

"It helps to swim with it."

"What did it reveal? For you?"

"Family," Whistle said. She pulled her white cover on and sat in the captain's chair. Behind her, on the beach, something moved. "Ready to go back?"

"Wait a minute." Celia leaned over the railing to see the large brown bodies of five horses appear from the island's wooded interior. The small herd moved in a bunch over the dunes and towards the surf. They had a serious, vigilant way about them. The larger adults craned their heads to watch the dunes. A foal stood pressed to a mare's side.

She imagined living on Bomb Island forever and following the horses on their slow patrols through the thick woods and lying down with them in little meadows they knew. She wanted to feel the soft tufts of fur that spotted the horses in strange patterns. Since she first learned of them from Derbier, she wished for these things. But the more she learned about the horses, the more she feared for them. Watching them move across the beach, she could only see them as victims. They were thin. They were hunted. There probably were no little meadows here where they could be at peace. This made her love them less.

What she had thought to be an image of living freedom was revealed to be something else. The horses were like the bomb, Celia thought. They'd been left in a disaster and allowed to decay. They were growing more stunted, more unstable, by the generation. Their use was symbolic. Their presence was alien. Their bodies were wasting away.

FOUR

fter everyone regrouped for a rice and bean dinner at camp
that night, Darlin and Reef secluded themselves in their
treehouse, and Whistle left to walk the beach. The water
grew dark and the mainland disappeared from view as the sun set
on the far side of the island. While they washed their plates in the
ocean, Fish asked Celia if she would use the Model 3.0 to ink the
sun into his foot.

"You're sure?" Celia asked.

"Totally."

"Then wash up," she said. She nodded to the black marsh mud
that streaked Fish's arms and legs. It had covered Darlin and Reef
as well.

When Celia climbed into Fish's treehouse with her backpack of
supplies, she saw he'd set out three enormous conches in the corners

of the room. The shells had been filled with wax and made into large candles. Behind the candles, on the wall of the treehouse, small mirrors had been installed to spread the yellow light. It was bright enough to read.

Two narrow bookshelves climbed the walls and held a large set of encyclopedias. A small cot covered in a brown woolen blanket was shoved against the wall to make the most of the tiny space, and a large screened window was cut into the wall above the bed.

It was a monk's house, Celia thought, but it was warm. "This is nice," she said. "I was worried I'd have to hold a flashlight."

"What do you think of these?" Fish showed her the sketches of the sun that he'd made on a torn piece of white cardboard. In one, the star was an eyeball wreathed in flames. In another, it was wrapped in vines. Fish had traced solar rays in thin lines that whorled like a thumbprint across the sun's surface.

"We can't do it like that," Celia said, and Fish frowned. "They're great, but they're too complex. It needs to be simple with a pen like this. See?" She pointed to the planets and stars that speckled her ankles. Most were just circles with solid rings of black ink. "This is some pro stuff," she said, and set the sun drawings on the floor carefully.

"What was your first one of?"

Celia laughed. "A cat." She turned her unbroken arm over to show a small, blurry smudge above her elbow. "Trust me. Keep it simple." She opened her backpack and began to set up her kit. "Draw it on your foot with the ballpoint when you're ready."

When Celia switched on the Model 3.0, the tattoo gun shook in her hand. She clamped her fingers around the head of the pen, and the machine quieted to a hum and held still. She pulled herself close to Fish and lifted his foot into her lap.

On the ball of his ankle, Fish had drawn a circle with a dot in the middle of it. "It's a symbol," he explained. "For the sun." Fresh pink scars stretched next to the design.

"Those are from the tiger?" Celia asked.

"Yeah."

"Then this will be nothing," she said. "Are you ready?"

"Yeah."

Fish watched Celia press the buzzing pen tip to his skin and trace the lines. The needle shot in and out of his skin. It stung, but the pain wasn't as sharp or sudden as a horsefly. It didn't burn like a sting from a wasp, but it was warm. At the twitch of Celia's hand, Fish's pain rose and fell. He sweat. He could feel the curve of the line she was following. Celia bore down, slightly harder. The needle jabbed muscle, and Fish grimaced.

It was the first time someone near his age had been on the island in years. It would have never happened if Reef, Whistle, even Nutzo had their way. He was proud he had invited her.

He saw his life in two parts. There was the time before he had kicked Sugar in the face, and the time after. Before, he had been at the whim of Whistle. He had been angry with her for not protecting him from Sugar. Angry with Reef for not protecting him from Jonathan, even though he never told any of them about what happened. When he kicked Sugar, he began the part of his life when he stopped waiting for others to do things for him. This was, he knew, the difference in children and adults.

"Almost done," Celia said. "You're doing great."

"Really?"

Celia was focused on the tattoo. Her bangs fell in front of her eyes, and she flicked them away. She lifted the pen, wiped ink with an alcoholic pad, and carefully filled the small circle that Fish said meant the sun. She wiped the tattoo once more with the alcohol. "Done."

Fish looked at the forever on his ankle. It looked more like an open eye than the sun. "Perfect," he said.

"You're in the club now. I just have to stab you like that kid said."

"Do what you must," Fish said. He turned his head away and clenched his jaw. Celia tickled the bottom of his foot with the fingertips that stuck from the end of her cast until he laughed. "Do you like it here?" he asked her, while he studied the tattoo.

"Sure."

"When the tiger's gone, you'll be welcome anytime."

"Oh yeah? I'm in the club now too?"

"Sure," Fish said. He was thinking of Reef and Darlin and how they sometimes stared at one another before they kissed. He had studied it. Before he kicked Sugar, he had thought the staring was necessary for making the kisses line up right, even though they often landed sideways. The lips slid off of each other and then rushed together again, but looking at Celia's lips now, Fish only felt the desire to be near her. As if he was rolling down a hill, being drawn to Celia by universal forces. He didn't need to measure.

There were times in Royals, when someone stared at him, that he felt his mole grow enormous and cover his face, but he didn't feel that way now. He didn't worry that his belly poked over his waistband or that one of his nipples was slightly larger than the other. Those were boy thoughts, he decided.

"What tattoo will you get next?"

"I don't know," Celia said. She saw the kiss in Fish's eyes like she had seen a hundred times before. She had seen it on the boy Mason's when he walked to his truck before all of this started. She wondered how different things might be if she had gone with him. They could be worse. She knew she should worry, but she felt light.

It felt good to be free of Adam, with miles of land and ocean between them. Adam, who knew that she had slept with Paul Francen, and the color of her bedroom walls, and where her spare key was kept. Fish only knew she liked tattoos and had a broken arm, and tomorrow she would leave with Darlin, and she would likely not come back. Derbier would never speak to her again, she was sure. This would all be a funny episode, she thought. Berny had them all the time.

"Boys are fun," her mother had told her. "Just make sure you have a plan to get home."

Fish laid his hand over Celia's on the deck of the treehouse. "I'm glad you're here," he said.

Celia closed her hand around Fish's. He was kind, she thought. She touched the clean line the razor had made on his scalp when he shaved his head for her party, and when Fish leaned for her, she closed her eyes and pressed her lips, gently, to his. Their faces brushed and bumped against one another. They kissed again. "Fish," she said.

"Yes."

"What would you tattoo on me?"

Fish leaned back to look at her. Dark bangs over bright eyes. He imagined an atom smashing across her cheeks. The gray shadow of an oat stalk behind her ear. "Where?"

"It depends on the design." She flipped the cardboard that Fish drew the suns on over and laid the ballpoint on top. "Draw." Fish leaned towards her again, but she pulled her head away. "Draw," she said.

They chose a tiger. It wasn't Sugar, Fish thought, but of course it was. He knew no others. Celia lay on her stomach on Fish's cot with her shirt folded beneath her and her back cast orange in the candle's glow. She rested her head on her good arm and watched Fish grimace as he began the long body of the tiger in profile on her left shoulder blade. She bumped him with her leg. "Don't look so serious," she said. "This is for fun."

Fish's face smoothed. He smiled. The pen rolled in long, smooth lines, and the ballpoint tiger appeared. The muscles in Celia's back moved, and the cat moved with them. He had drawn Sugar with his head inclined and his mouth slightly agape. It was the way he looked when he was stalking, his body low. The tiger's head rested on Celia's shoulder like the cap of a white sand dune. They found an old mirror of Reef's, and Fish held it over Celia's back so she could see.

"Can you do it?" she asked.

"Yeah."

"Then do it. Start at the bottom so you don't smudge the pen."

Fish's hands were sweating when he switched on the Model 3.0, covered the head in ink, and pressed it to the tiger's back foot. Little bumps rose in a wave across Celia's skin. He followed them with his eyes until they disappeared into the jeans she wore.

"You alright?" He lifted the tattoo gun. Sweat appeared on Celia's skin in tiny, silver orbs. Dew in a spider's web. The air in the treehouse was stifling.

"Too deep," she said. "Just under the skin. Like the lemon."

Fish moved the shell candles closer. He leaned close to Celia's back and traced out the tiger's shape, wiping when the ink pooled and ran. The needle moved across Celia's skin in slow drags. It passed between freckles and over tiny, pale hairs. When his weight shifted and the needle bit into Celia, she sucked in air, and he wiped the blood away.

"I saw the horses," she said.

"How are you going to save them?"

"I guess they're going to have to shoot them all," Celia said. Fish laughed, but she didn't. "It's probably what they'll do. One day."

"I don't think so."

"You're probably right. They'll just leave them to inbreed until the horse flu kills them. Or their water goes bad."

"What are you talking about?" Fish asked.

"Nobody in Georgia cares about these horses. If they did, they'd take care of them."

She must have seen the skeletons in the dunes, Fish thought. "Have you seen the mansion?"

"I'm not into old houses."

"There's a big field there. I guess it's got the best grass on the island because the horses stay all day. I've seen them walk up the marble stairs. Through the doorway even."

"You're missing the point," she said. "They shouldn't be here."

Fish knew she was right. No one had come to the island to see the horses in years. There had been a photographer once, a young woman that Whistle knew, but she abandoned the project. There was no tiger on the island then, but she found the remains of horses who had died with their tails snagged in the brush, or their bodies stuck between tree trunks, or swallowed up in the marsh that waves just like a field of grass. Ponies of the plains. The planters brought them.

"I'll show you where they have it good. They're broken into families, sort of. The rich horses stay with the grass at the mansion, and the poor horses walk the beach. I saw a horse eat an oyster once."

"What?"

"It broke the shell with its hoof and licked out the meat."

"Gross."

"And they eat bird eggs. They'll knock a nest from a tree. For the iron."

The tattoo tiger was taking shape. Fish traced the tip of its tongue, then the flat nose, the outline of Sugar's wide head. Thin black lines over a blush of blood. His fingers were numb from the buzz of the tool.

"You were born here?" she asked.

"When I was a baby, I lived in Atlanta."

"Lots to do there."

"I don't think I'm going."

"You could always come back," she said. "After Sugar's gone. The island isn't going anywhere. You could come back and give tours."

"Would you come?"

"I don't know where I'll be," she said. "I'll live with my mom for a while. I don't even know where she is."

"We should just take care of Sugar ourselves. Me and Reef. Self-defense."

"Don't be stupid."

"What do you mean?"

"Let Whistle handle this. She thinks Sugar is like her pet or son or something, and it's fucked up, but she's dealing with it. Give her some time, then come back. Be cool."

"Be cool," Fish said. She thought he couldn't do it. "I've got a mohawk now."

"What's with the camera?" she asked.

Fish had moved the handheld to one of the bookshelves, and it stared down on them with its single black eye. One-eyed blackbird, Fish thought. "Just something I found."

"After the party. It was in the woods."

"Yeah."

"What like you had it stashed?"

Fish dipped the needle in the ink and laid it to Celia's back with care. He drew over his line, watching the tip of the machine make its cut, just a breath beneath the skin. "It wasn't like that."

"I don't care if you took it."

"It's just some dumb thing," Fish said. He wondered if Celia knew Jonathan. If she had seen the videos, she wouldn't have asked about the camera. If she had seen the videos, she wouldn't have kissed him.

"Okay."

"It's doesn't have your dad on it or anything."

"Okay."

"Why is he like that?"

"Who? My dad?" Celia lifted her head to look at him. "That's what you want to talk about?"

"I don't care," Fish said. He was thinking of the things Jonathan had told him about the girls he knew in Savannah, where, he said, "anyone can get laid." An image of Jonathan kissing Celia forced itself into Fish's brain. In the dream, he snatched her hair and pulled her tight against him. He shoved his hand down the front of her shorts.

"He's an angry guy, I guess," Celia said. "He just is. Ouch. Ow!"

"Sorry." Fish wiped Celia's back where it bled from the thick, black stripes that stretched two inches from the ink tiger's back to its belly. Fish had to pass over the stripes again and again to fill them. The details of the tiger were becoming hard for him to see on Celia's irritated skin. A drop of blood swelled then rolled down her back, and he wiped it away.

"John-Elvis saw the deputies take him, and he hadn't been back to the house. Shit, that hurt. I think you blew it out. Let me see."

Fish held the mirror over her bleeding back. "You talked to John-Elvis?"

"I heard him talking to Whistle." She looked at the tattoo in the mirror, and she pursed her lips.

"Did he say how Derbier was? He can breathe and everything?" They might come for him, Fish thought, if he had broken something vital. If they knew who he was.

"He looked like he was breathing fine to me at Darlin's."

"That was my first fight," Fish said.

"Fight? He got sprayed and you kicked him. It's like I told you before, you didn't have to do that."

"He was getting back up!"

Fish felt the blood swell in his shoulders. It embarrassed him that his manhood wasn't clear to her, and the only other option seemed to be that she thought of him as a child. If she had seen him fight off Sugar, Fish thought, she would understand him better.

"Fights don't impress me," Celia said. She turned away from the mirror and laid her head on his bed. "Derbier gets into fights all the time, so don't feel special about it."

"What makes you feel special?" Fish cupped Celia's backside with his hand. He squeezed the hard muscle.

"What the fuck are you doing?" Celia sat up. She covered her breasts with her arm. She raised her cast arm like a club.

"What?"

"What the fuck, what? Keep your hands to yourself."

"Be careful," Fish said. Thin, red lines were trailing down Celia's side. He reached for her back with the alcohol wipe, and she knocked his hand away. "Turn the fuck around so I can put on my shirt."

"You'll get blood on it. Look, I'm sorry. It's okay."

"Get out of here!"

"You want me to leave?"

"Go!"

Fish climbed onto the ladder, but kept his head inside the treehouse. "I'm sorry."

"Get!"

"I didn't mean to come at you like that. Just let me explain."

Celia reached into her bag and pulled out the mace John-Elvis gave her, but she fumbled the can and dropped it on the floor. "Get out!" she shouted.

"Fine!" Fish shouted back. "Whatever! Okay!" He leapt from the top of the treehouse ladder and rolled when he hit the dirt. He looked back to see if Celia would follow him or was, possibly, worried that he had hurt himself, but he only saw her naked arm, ripping the burlap curtain-door over the treehouse's opening. It was dusk, and the mosquitos nagged him.

"Fish," Whistle called to him. She had rebuilt the cook fire and sat at its edge. Light gray smoke came from the fire in plumes.

"I'm fine," he said. He didn't know how much she had heard.

"Come here," she said.

"I'm okay!" he shouted. Fish climbed into Nutzo's abandoned treehouse and took what he needed from the old man's things. The heavy flashlight, the spare lighter, the half-sized shovel that was sharp enough to clear brush. He stuffed it all into a cloth bag and carried it with him, back down the ladder.

"It's too late to go out," Reef said.

Fish didn't answer. He had already told them he was fine, and he had already heard all of their plans to run away to Atlanta, but he had his own plans. He let out of the camp at a run, pushed through a wall of dark fronds, and disappeared on a narrow path through the woods that he knew.

He could hear Reef running after him, crashing through the undergrowth. Fish switched off the flashlight and slipped behind an oak. He felt a sagging hollowness in his chest when he thought of the way Celia had sat up, so quickly, when he'd touched her.

How disgusted she looked. But the island's lesson was clear. When there was a challenge, it was more action, not less, that changed things. He crouched on the ground and waited until Reef's large feet pounded by, then he called out from his hiding place. "Reef!"

The big man stopped. "Where are you?" he shouted.

"I'm going to kill the tiger."

"Not alone! You need to come back. It's not safe out here."

Fish could hear him moving through the brush toward his voice. Then he heard him trip and curse.

Fish slipped further into the dark. In the wooded middle of the island, even a full moon couldn't light the forest floor. "Will you help me?" he asked. "Then we can stay."

"We can't stay," Reef said.

"You won't help me?"

"Come back to camp!"

Fish left Reef stumbling and shouting while he crept back to the trail and then jogged for the southern marsh. He would do it himself.

In Fish's treehouse, Celia stuffed her things back into her bag and pulled her shirt, awkwardly, over her cast and head. She had finished crying and now her face and back stung. When she kicked Fish's bed against the wall, the camera fell off of its shelf and crashed to the floor. She picked up the handheld. She lifted it to the shelf, then took it back and thumbed the power on. The small, flip-out screen filled with color and light in the dark treehouse.

Fish's face appeared on the screen. He was shirtless and in a bathing suit. It looked like he was on a dock. He smiled. "Is it recording?"

"Asshole," Celia said.

"Shut up," a boy's voice said off-screen. "This is an interview for scientific purposes," the boy said. "First question: What is your real name?"

"My name is Fish."

FIVE

The sand on Bomb Island moved aside for the steel shovel, and Fish threw it over his shoulder into the dark. After a foot of sand, the ground grew firm and wet. After two hours, he stood in a rectangular pit three feet deep. His mouth was dry. The skin on his hands was torn. The tiger trap would need to be at least two feet deeper to work, and even then, Sugar might just leap out.

After he had run from the camp, he had retrieved the cooler of explosives. His plan was to cover the pit, then hang bait above it and wait in a nearby tree for Sugar to fall in. To kill the tiger, he would light and throw one of the bottle bombs into the pit. He hoped it would only take one. He didn't know what would happen when he set fire to one of the six-inch fuses that stuck from the bottles' stoppered mouths.

Fish climbed out of the hole and sat on the fresh dirt and stared at the explosives, imagining the moment he would light one. He should test them, he thought. He lifted one of the bottles from the cooler. He brought it close to his face. There were layers of different materials inside, light and dark. They didn't look damaged.

"What you doing, Fisherman?" The rasping voice came from nowhere.

Fish acted as if he hadn't heard. He lowered the bottle, carefully, back into the cooler and shut the lid. He had chosen a wide patch of sand beneath an oak to make his trap. Under the moon, he could see well. The brush pressed in on all sides of the little clearing. There was no one there. He made himself very still and listened, but he only heard the muffled pounding of waves coming ashore. He was close to the beach. "Nutz," he said. "That you?"

A thin old man stepped from the brush. His hair was a close-cropped, silver field, and his beard was a wiry mess. His lips were cracked. He wore a loincloth and carried a wizard's staff. "What do you want with that stuff?"

"I'm going to kill Sugar."

Nutzo walked to the edge of the pit Fish had dug. He was wearing a mask on the back of his head with large, open almond eyes outlined with white paint. Bright yellow flames rose from the eyes and made points on the mask's brow. The white mouth was cut into a sharp, pointed frown. This was, Nutzo told him once, how a group of villagers in India learned to protect themselves from tigers.

The village was losing ten souls a year. The government put out a bounty. They set out human dummies connected to buried car batteries. They offered poisoned meat. The attacks continued. Only the masks made a difference. Tigers prefer to ambush from behind, and the masks kept watch.

Nutzo tested the pit's depth with his driftwood staff. "This is three feet too shallow."

"Okay."

"You cut your hair. You—oh!" Fish had wrapped him in a hug.

"Why didn't you tell us you were going?" Fish asked with his head against the old man's chest. He smelled like low tide.

Nutzo lowered himself to the sand. "I had an argument with Whistle. I had to get away."

"About what?"

"The tiger."

"She said she'll get rid of him," Fish said, "but Reef wants to leave for Atlanta now. It could take her weeks for find someplace to take Sugar. And then how long to trap him? If they could even do it."

"Traps take time."

Fish looked at his shallow tiger pit. The bottom was lit by the dimming beam of the flashlight. It would probably take him until day to dig the trap properly. By then, Reef would be gone. He should have been digging since he found the dynamite.

"Maybe I'll just throw the bottles at him."

Nutzo sat in silence, staring into the brush with his brow furrowed. His beard twitched. He spat something out. A sunflower seed.

"You think it's too dangerous," Fish said.

"It's dangerous."

"Maybe if Reef knew you were back, he would stay."

"No."

"He's worried about you. He thinks you're dead. Or in Atlanta."

Nutzo grunted.

"So talk to him." Fish pushed Nutzo's shoulder. "With the dynamite, if we were all three of us working together, we could do it easy."

"It's not easy. Reef is leaving with Darlin," Nutzo said. "Will you go with him?"

"No. I don't know."

"Let's think about it now, and I will think too, and we will decide what to do." Nutzo straightened his back and rested his hands in his lap. He closed his eyes, and his face relaxed. His breath was smooth and measured.

Fish sat next to him, staring into the pit. He listened for the tiger and heard nothing. His new tattoo burned on his ankle. Even if he killed the tiger and stayed on the island, he didn't think he would see Celia again. But if he could kill Sugar, who knew what would happen? Anything seemed possible. He listened to the ocean, imagining a future where he wore normal clothes and drove a long, silver car. Whistle had told him about the universities and museums in Atlanta. He didn't want to leave. Not now. Not because of Sugar.

"If you kill the tiger, it will hurt Whistle," Nutzo said.

"I know that."

Sugar was no pet to Fish. He was thrilled by the tiger, but in the two years Sugar had lived on the island, Fish had never felt love between them. When the tiger was a cub, he swatted and squalled, then he grew elusive. He disappeared often. It seemed that Sugar had claimed the island and had, until recently, tolerated Fish and the others living on it.

"She may leave."

"Would you stay?" Fish asked him.

"I would stay," Nutzo said.

"I would stay too."

"Then let's dig."

Together, Fish and Nutzo widened the trap to four feet. They dug until, when he stood in the hole, Fish could no longer reach to dump sand over its edge. They took small sips from Nutzo's canteen and ate from a leather bag of jerky and pecans that he kept on his hip, and then they planted stakes of sharpened bamboo on the bottom of the trap.

They had made play versions of these traps before Sugar came to the island, when there had been more people. Fish remembered leading Sara by the hand on the beach until she stepped on a beach towel and slipped into a shallow sand hole. They never used the traps for hunting. They were too dangerous to have around. What Fish and Nutzo made in the clearing was the real deal. Something Fish had never considered before. It was simple and ugly. The fall, humorless, and at the bottom, the long points of green wood stakes.

They laid dead palm fronds across the wide mouth of the pit, and over these they threw leaves, sand, and moss. Finally, they laid a broken limb that was the diameter of a man's arm on top of the trap's false floor, and it didn't fall through. It was done.

Fish hid the cooler of dynamite under a limb at the base of the tree and slouched, exhausted with Nutzo on the sand. His mind began to list, but excitement kept him alert. The night was warm. He savored the relief of leaning against the cool trunk of the tree after the hard digging. It felt good to work with the old man.

Nutzo cleaned Fish's damaged hands and wrapped them in gauze, but he was still watching the brush. "He might have seen us working."

"Sugar?"

"He's smart."

"How will we get him here?"

"We'll fish for bait." Nutzo tied off the gauze in a knot over Fish's knuckles.

Fish wished he could show the trap to Celia. The embarrassment of what had happened at camp made him feel heavy and sick. "I need to go back," he said.

"What for?"

"I have to apologize to someone."

"Whistle?"

"No. A girl, Celia."

"Why would you bring a girl here? To the tiger." It was the first time in the night Nutzo seemed angry with him.

"She needed a place to go."

"She should go as soon as possible. If you care about her, tell her to go. Tell them all. No one should be on this island while the tiger is here. Do whatever you can to get them to go."

"You want me to come back?"

"No," Nutzo said. "I want you to be safe." He squeezed Fish's shoulder. "You have always been able to make your own decisions. Be thoughtful, Fish."

SIX

I t was over a mile back to the camp. Fish's feet were calloused, but his bones were starting to ache. His skin squeaked over loose, sugar sand. It was dark. The owls called, but the turkeys hadn't begun to cry. Dawn was still a way off.

Whistle sat by the cook fire in her usual place. Her hair was down and fell to her lower back. It covered her like a sheet. "Come sit," she said when she saw Fish.

Reef sat across the fire from her. "You look terrible," he said. "Where were you?" He was propped up against a stump and red around the eyes. "You ran off on me."

"You're one to talk."

Reef only waved his hand, too tired to argue.

There was water boiling. The mugs were lined on the sand. It could have been any morning on the island. Fish's legs felt sluggish and thick. He sat by the fire. He planned to sit there until Celia and Darlin woke, then he would apologize and give Nutzo's message. He fought the urge to sleep.

"Where did you go?" Reef asked.

"You know where I went."

"What? For the cooler?"

"Why do you need to kill Sugar?" Whistle asked.

"He's trying to kill me. Reef, tell her."

"He's a danger to you, so let's remove the danger. Go with Reef for now. You won't be in Atlanta a month before I send for you. Let me handle this the right way."

"He's not just a danger to me, he's a danger to everyone. None of us should be here."

"Then we'll all go," Whistle said. "I'll go with you to Atlanta, and then I'll come back to remove Sugar."

Fish considered this. Going to Atlanta with Whistle would give Nutzo more than enough time to lure Sugar to the trap, but it would mean leaving him alone on the island to do it. And if Nutzo did kill Sugar, and Whistle found out, what would she do? He didn't know if she would still come back for him. No one could make her. Atlanta was so far away. It would be easy, he thought, to be trapped there.

"Killing Sugar is not going to make our lives better," Whistle said.

"One month," Reef said. "If you don't like it, I'll bring you back."

"You don't have a license," Fish said.

"I'll get you back. One month."

"And you would come with us?" Fish asked Whistle.

She nodded. "Yes."

"Alright," Fish said. If he could lead them all away, maybe that would be enough.

"Alright," Whistle said. "You don't have to be a killer to be an adult," she said. "To be a man."

"I know that."

"What did you feel when you kicked that man in Royals?"

"Derbier?" Fish said.

"Celia's father."

"I didn't feel anything. He's a bad guy. I didn't do anything wrong."

"No one is saying you did," Reef said.

"You didn't feel anything?" Whistle asked.

"I wanted him to leave us alone."

"And then what happened?"

"He followed us to Darlin's. It's not my fault that he's an angry, violent guy. I stood up to him. Like Nutzo."

"No," Whistle said. "You're right that you can't control his actions, but you might anticipate them, and you can control yourself. There are other ways to protect the people you care about."

"When I told you that story about Nutz driving over the car," Reef said. "That shouldn't have happened like that. We should have just left."

"And then Whistle doesn't get her books? Because some jerk wanted to use them to lure her to him? How is that right? Why should we just walk away and give him what isn't his? Not when we don't have to. We don't have to give him anything. When Nutzo drove over his car, he let him know he couldn't mess with us."

Fish stared into the ocean. He squinted. Something bobbing in the water had caught his eye. It was a small, white thing. It was being pushed onto the beach by the tide, and seemed to glow in the soft light of the fire.

"No," Reef said. "We just pissed that guy off. And it ended badly."

Fish stood and walked to the tide line. He pointed his flashlight at the white thing at his feet. It was the omen.

"It washed up hours ago," Whistle said. "Leave it. It's a pelican, not an omen."

"We saw it on the trail."

"Then it shouldn't be a mystery to you."

"You just left it here?"

"Fish, if anything, this bird is a good omen. You're safe. Celia and Darlin are safe. You came back. Let this unfortunate pelican be a reminder that we should work to avoid death and violence and celebrate the time we have. Do you know what happened after that man in Atlanta shot me?"

"We came here."

"That's right. We adapted. We didn't stay in Atlanta and hunt that man down. We didn't kill him. We found new love. We saved the energy we might have wasted on that man, and we made a home." Whistle poured tea in five mugs. "No one is waiting to tally who hurt who the most at the end of this life," she said. "There's only the love we share now and the good that comes from it. Anything else is wasted time."

Fish pushed the pelican away from the beach with his foot.

"Don't touch it!" Reef said.

Fish heard the squeaking of a ladder and saw Celia and Darin climb down from Nutzo's tree, and he ran to them. "Celia, I'm so sorry."

"Forget it," she said. "It's done."

Darlin walked past them to join Whistle and Reef at the fire.

"I wasn't thinking," he said.

"Of course you were. You wanted to touch me, so you did. It's simple. It's just not like that with us is all. Not for me."

"What will you do?"

Celia stepped around Fish. "I'm going to sit by this pretty fire, and then I'm going home."

"What about the tattoo?"

"It was a good start. Thank you. I'll have it finished sometime."

"Come over here, ass-grabber," Reef called to Fish from the fire.

"Jesus," Celia said. "Shut the fuck up, huh?"

They sat around the fire and drank their tea, waiting for the sun to rise. No one had slept. They were all delirious. Celia's hair was bent into antlers. Reef burned his hand on his tea. The taste of an orange. It was all too funny. They talked about the city while they waited for the sun.

"My cousin's wife," Reef said. "She's got five little white dogs in a two-bedroom place. Five. That's where we're going. I figure we get there, we get our feet under us, we get out of the dog house." He worked his hand like a puppet and yapped over the fire. Everyone gripped their sides.

"Is there anything you're looking forward to?" Darlin asked Whistle.

"The people," Whistle said, and Reef snorted. "I do have some friends there that I would like to see," she said. "Some that might even come back with us when things are better."

"Who?" Fish asked.

"Only old friends. There's a woman I've kept up with through letters. She has two boys. We could meet them."

"You would bring them here?"

"Maybe. If they wanted to be here. Some people need another place to be. We have the room. And the tours will continue."

"I saw Nutzo," Fish said.

Reef brayed. "He was just out there this whole time. I knew it." He lay on the ground, holding Darlin's leg and laughing, until she too laughed and from there it spread until they were all crying. "He was right here," Reef wheezed. "We looked everywhere."

"Was he hurt?" Whistle asked. She was wiping tears from her eyes.

"No," Fish said. "He was fine. I don't think he'll come back to camp for a while."

"What did he say to you?"

Fish sat in the old man's straight-backed, meditative pose. He took several deep breaths.

Reef began to giggle.

"Be thoughtful, Fish."

Whistle smiled, but she didn't laugh. "That's all he said?"

"He said you fought. But it's over now. He wasn't angry. I told him you changed your mind about Sugar."

"What did you say? Did you believe you?"

She appeared to Fish in the form of a feeble old woman. With her hair fallen in front of her face, the scar was a dark groove cut into her skin. She hunched under her quilt alone. "Yeah," Fish said. "He thought it was a good idea."

"He doesn't want to come live with five tiny white dogs?!" Reef laughed. "You will never get that man to the city. It's hard enough to get him into a pair of shorts."

"He'll be okay," Fish said.

The laugher trickled in and out, and then it grew quiet around the fire. Darlin and Reef leaned against each other and dozed. Celia lay on her side in the sand with her back against a bench log and her cast cradled to her chest. Whistle sat very still with her eyes closed.

Fish leaned against a log with his back to the water. When he felt he couldn't keep his eyes open, he got up and washed in the ocean. He scrubbed his cheeks with sand. He slapped his face and sat back against his log looking into the dark of the woodline and listening for the tiger. He watched the sky over the trees change from black to blue.

While they laughed and drank tea by a fire, Nutzo was alone. He was probably fishing in one of the mud creeks. Fish imagined himself looking through Sugar's eyes. It would be so easy to creep through the thick marsh grass. He saw Nutzo's bare shoulders and thin brown neck. The wooden face on the back of his head.

It wouldn't stop me, Fish thought. He didn't think it would stop Sugar for long, and he worried. He was lonesome for the old man's company. He reassured himself that getting everyone off of the island was a mission as important as springing the trap. It was the most important part. He stared into the woods.

"Fish," Whistle said. She opened her quilt and made a place for him. Everyone else was asleep. When he lay beside her, she wrapped her arm around his shoulders and kissed the top of his head. "Our lives are changing for a little while."

"Yeah."

"I found this on the ground." She handed him the driftwood necklace he had worn to the party.

"Thank you." He hadn't noticed it was missing. He slipped it over his head. "I'll be more careful with it."

"I love you," she said.

"I love you too."

"I will always be on your side."

"I know that. Is everything alright?"

"I think it will be. It may do us some good to be away for a little while," she said.

"Maybe."

"You've made friends here." She nodded to Celia and Darlin. "You'll see them again."

"I guess."

"I'm worried about you, Fish. You have so much anger in you. I've been dreaming bad things."

"I saw the omen."

"I'm not talking about that."

"Well, maybe you should be," Fish said. "We all saw it. Don't act like I'm crazy."

"You're not crazy," Whistle said. "But interpreting these things isn't simple. Sometimes we imagine connections that aren't there. We see the pelican in the water, but we don't know how it's linked to us. It might be on its way to someplace else. It floats."

"It's here for us."

"Okay. Why do you think it's here?"

"You mean why do we have bad luck?"

"If you like."

"We must have done something wrong."

"Have we?"

"We brought Sugar here."

"I did that," she said. "And I didn't see the bird on the trail or in my dreams."

He didn't want to believe the omen had come because he stole the handheld from Jonathan. What did the birds care about it? "Maybe this whole island is haunted."

"What does that mean?"

"It means bad things happen here. Those planes crashed into each other and dropped the bomb here. Two little planes in the middle of the night. Why did they have to hit here?"

"I don't know."

"And the horses. They're trapped here."

"Yes."

"Why did you stay here when everyone left? All the people you came here with."

"I wanted to. I had already changed so much about my life to be here. I sold my house. I left a job I enjoyed and the last of my blood family."

"Why here?"

"I thought it would be quiet. I thought it would be fun. Some of us needed a place to go that was private. I convinced them that if we built something here, we would have the time and space to grow into better versions of ourselves, versions that we would never know if we stayed in the city, where it felt like a lot of things were already decided for us. We had our professions and our problems, and we were being pushed along our trajectories until their end. Does that make sense?"

"You needed to get away."

"Some of us had troubles, but others were simply bored or curious. We came here because we wanted to live differently. I was convinced it would be worth any discomfort, and I was very proud of everyone for taking that risk. I was grateful to not take it alone."

Fish had been five when they came to the island. He remembered that John-Elvis took them across the sound in a sailboat, like the one he'd scraped barnacles from just a couple days ago. He didn't remember much else, besides a moment with Sara.

They had stood on the deck of the boat and looked out at the twisted, dead trees on the ocean-facing beach. "The trees look hungry," his mother said. "I hope they don't eat you up."

"You can go anywhere you want," Whistle said. "You're not trapped here like the horses and the bomb."

"I know."

"Where do you want to go?"

"I want to be here. I don't want everything to change," he said. He looked to where Celia lay on the sand. She had the hood on her sweatshirt pulled over her head and looked, from here, like a small pile of clothes. She seemed to be asleep. He wondered if she regretted kissing him.

A turkey screamed, late, into the thin blue air.

"Do you really think other people would come back here with us from Atlanta?"

"Yes," Whistle said. "It will probably be hard for them at first. You don't remember, but it was hard for us too. I'll need your help showing them how to live here, if they come. And on the tours. In a couple years, you'll be leading them, if you like."

"I'd like that." Fish lay on the quilt with a wadded t-shirt under his head and looked into the glittering coal bed. In Atlanta, he thought, they would use microwaves to make their tea. They would ride enormous city buses filled with people they had never seen before, and when they came back Sugar would be gone.

"I'm proud of you, Fish," Whistle said, but the boy was quiet and still. She sat in the circle of sleepers, listening to them breathe. She closed her eyes for what felt like a second, and when she opened them again the sky was lighter and Sugar was at her side.

The tiger was curled like a housecat on the sand. Its paws were caked in black mud. Tiny scars covered Sugar's body, appearing as blips in his smooth, white coat. Places where oysters and boar tusks and horse hooves had cut him.

Whistle sat between Fish and Sugar. She had hoped that on Bomb Island she could build a life for them that would be free of the deadends and cages that Atlanta might have channeled them into. For a time, she had, but the sound was too narrow to insulate them forever. They couldn't be safely contained. She was their mother, and she was a stranger. They had both grown beyond her control.

Her plan for a utopia had been marked by abandonment. She decided, there on the beach, that it was for the best. She had been wrong, all those years before, when she thought that isolation was the answer to the brutality and sickness she found in Atlanta. Her vison of pursuing the highest expressions of personal freedom was tainted by fear. They had been driven out of the city in fear, and they were being driven back to it now. Fear had made her tight-fisted with her lovers, and they had fled to the woods or the arms of others. To Sugar, the fear was an intoxicant, and to Fish it seemed a challenge. She saw him thrashing against it.

Where she had once believed, privately, that surviving her husband's bullet meant she was destined to be a bastion to the hopeless, now she wasn't so sure. Mainland rationalism had found her here as slowly as if it had pursued her, at a walk, from the city. It had eaten away at the wards she believed existed on the island—spiritual barriers that emanated from the bomb and allowed for hope, second chances, and spiritual self-sufficiency.

She remembered—she knew—that she had brought Sugar to the island, but for the past year she began to think he had appeared here as a specter, molded by the spirits of vengeful maroons and doomed horses. He was a force sent to remind them all: We cannot hide from what hunts us. We have to meet it.

Slowly, she reached out her arms to her children. She held her left palm an inch over Fish's head and her right over the tiger's. She felt the heat rising from them. She felt their three hearts beating in unison. She wept in silence. She smiled and buried her feet in the sand and made herself into a conduit. She wanted, always, to feel love moving through her.

PART THREE

ONE

The sheriff held Derbier overnight in a windowless white room. The bed was without sheets and had, instead, a roll of paper bolted to the foot of the frame. His throat hurt from where the island boy had kicked him, and he pounded on the walls of the room, demanding water, until a man pounded his fist on the other side and shouted for him to shut it. Derbier lay on the bed in silence, watching yellow bruises appear on his ribs and stomach. His left eye was swollen closed. He touched the skin beneath it gingerly and winced.

After he'd been charged and promised to appear in court, he called Rodney Pickens from the basement of the jail and rode back to Royals on the edge of three tallboys, a pack of salted nuts, and a red Gatorade bought from a gas station. Pickens was not a friend, but Derbier's sole employee, and the only person in a three-hour radius that he could coerce into picking him up.

"It was freezing in there," Derbier said.

Pickens switched the A/C's loud blower off. "I can't stay around if we're not fishing."

Derbier drank his beer and stared through the passenger window of Rod's truck. One of his orange promotional hats was folded up and behind Pickens's windshield with the manufacturer's stickers still on it. He tried to roll down the window to feel the warm air on his face, but the crank handle spun in its hole.

"It's broke," Pickens said. "Like me."

Derbier had missed two charters while he was being held in the jail. He hadn't been able to call them to cancel, and he hadn't told Pickens. At the height of his business in Savannah, he paid two captains year round. In the summer, that doubled. Some weeks they went out every day. In Royals, there was barely enough work for one boat. The marina bustled with locals but attracted few tourists looking to fish. Those that did come, came for the bomb.

"You alright? I just need to make a little more is all. If we're going to keep doing this."

"We'll talk about it tomorrow," Derbier said. He set his empty can on the floorboard. The next beer sprayed when he opened it. "Shit." He reached for the window crank again, then opened the truck's door to the wind and the highway and let the beer run off.

"Jesus, man. You don't have a charter?"

"The summer's just started. I've got plenty of work. Don't worry about it. I'll call you tomorrow."

"I'm serious."

They passed a boarded-up gas station and turned onto the crushed-shell road that led to Royals through deep acres of planted pines. The brush had been burned away, and the trees stood like soldiers on scorched earth. Derbier watched the lanes between the pines for deer, but there was only clear day. Then, all at once, the trees fell off on the left side of the road and the marsh began. Royals clung to the edge of the brown salt river. The marina's green tin roof and the tall I-beams of the boat lift overlooked the grid of houses called Sea Wall.

"Goddamn," Pickens said when they reached Derbier's place. "The pharaoh's pyramid is in your driveway."

The doors to the house were unlocked, but Derbier couldn't find his keys. They weren't in his truck, which was parked where he'd left it. "You want to do something?" he asked Pickens. "My keys are loose." He knew he didn't remember taking them out of the ignition, but he still retraced his steps from the door of his truck to the house, through the filthy kitchen and out the back door. He only glanced into his destroyed bedroom and came out, again, through the back door to the garage where Celia had sprayed him. He found nothing. The blackened spring skeleton of his mattress lay on the ground, looking like a medieval torture device. He imagined strapping the island boy to it and dragging him through town.

"What about my property?" he'd asked the deputies after they'd gotten him into the car.

"You'll have to make a report."

Pickens kicked around in the grass for Derbier's keys for a few minutes, then walked back to his truck and lit a cigarette. "Call me tomorrow," he said.

"You want to help me out here?" Derbier called. He was digging through the truck's center console for the third time. "Fucking boat keys are gone too."

"Might be that somebody's got them."

Derbier slammed the door of the truck and stomped to where Pickens was smoking, half in his truck and half out. "You know something I don't?"

"I can't help today."

"Why the hell not?"

"I just can't is all," Pickens said. "I'll talk to you tomorrow."

"Well what am I supposed to do with that? You said you wanted to work, well we can't work without the keys to the boat."

"We got a boat. We got my boat," Pickens said. "Let me pick up the slack."

Derbier kicked the front tire of Pickens's truck. "Get out of here."

"What?"

"I said get out of here before I knock your head off."

"What the hell did you say?" Pickens swung his feet to the ground and made to get out of the truck, but Derbier shoved him back inside the cab.

"Get out of here. And don't come asking me for work."

"I just drove thirty minutes to spring you from jail, dipshit."

Derbier only walked back to his house.

"Hey, we've got business," Pickens called after him. "Hey!" He snatched Debier's hat from the dash and threw it across the yard. "Hey, asshole!"

Derbier picked the topmost can off of the silver pyramid and pitched it into the grill of Pickens's truck. He threw another that skidded off the windshield and left a run of piss-colored beer sliding down the glass.

"You're busted, man," Pickens shouted. He slammed the door to his truck and spun his tires over the grass backing out of the yard.

Derbier threw another beer into the truck door. The heavy can, still half-full, cut into the metal and left a dent. "Bust that."

"Are you serious?" Pickens lurched over the shallow ditch and into the road, then drove the roaring truck back over the ditch on a collision course with Derbier. The bigger man ran for the front door, and Pickens plowed his truck through the pyramid of beer cans and into the side of Derbier's house. The brush guard bit into the red brick and crushed it. When the truck reversed, half of the wall tore away.

Derbier stood in his yard and listened to the sound of Pickens's truck racing on the blacktop highway. He leaned his head against the brick. Yellow insulation was poking from the hole in his house. He walked inside and found the kitchen phone on the stained vinyl floor. It had been ripped from the wall. He plugged the phone in and dialed his ex-wife.

Bernice's voicemail was brief. Her voice, festive. "Please," she said, "leave a detailed message."

"Bernice," he said. "Bernice, pick up. Celia?" He knew they were on the other end of the line in Savannah, laughing at him. He waited for someone to answer. "Bernice!" A beep sounded and a machine's voice spoke. "This recorded message has ended. Goodbye."

He collapsed into the twin bed in the guest room, where Celia had stayed for the last two weeks. The smell of the strawberry shampoo he'd bought her stuck in his throat. It was too sweet. He wadded his own stinking t-shirt beneath his head to block it out, and fell into a deep and immediate sleep.

When he woke, the house was dark, and he was still alone. It was four in the morning. Celia's duffle bag was open on the floor. She had never unpacked it into the low, white dresser that Derbier had bought for the room. Once, he hoped Celia would stay here as much as she did in Savannah, but this was only the fourth time she had come to Royals.

When he'd picked his daughter up from the Savannah house, he'd worn a new white shirt that'd he'd bought from an outlet on the way. He combed his thinning hair with his fingers in the driveway while he waited for her to come outside and tried not to think of the many lowcountry boils he'd served on long, wooden tables in the front yard of the house during better days.

Celia had brought next to nothing. Just the duffle and her backpack. "What's that?" he asked when he saw the green cast on her arm.

"I slammed it in a door."

"How did you do that?"

"In a hurry," she'd said.

He never understood what Celia hated so much about him. He had never cheated on her mother. Besides the spankings he gave her as a small child, he had never touched her in anger. Or at least he never hit her. She hadn't had to endure the boots and belts and backhands his father had subjected him to, and he told her as much when she screamed at him through the guest room door. Long gone were the days she would sit on his lap and show him what scribbles she had made over Pretty Pretty Princess coloring books.

Derbier usually rose and left the house before dawn to stock the boat's livewell with shrimp or mullet and hose off any residual mud or blood from the inside of the boat's smooth white hull. When he returned in the afternoon, Celia would often still be asleep, or else she was at Darlin's smoking reefer. At night, she locked herself in the guest room and drew in a notebook. He found the sketchbook on the floor and flipped through the sketches. The images were grotesque.

Derbier curled his lips at the skinless, muscular shapes of female bodies in wide sunhats. An alien woman in a hiked-up wedding dress lay on the hood of a flying saucer with her large, oval eye squeezed shut while a skeleton buried its face between her legs. He felt himself becoming aroused and tossed the book beneath the bed, disgusted. He didn't know where she was or what he would say to her when he found out.

The house's only toilet was filled to the brim with brown water and wads of toilet paper, so Derbier stepped into the night to pee. He was leaned against a tree, relieving himself, when the phone rang inside the house, and he ran to answer it with his pants unbuckled and sagging.

"Hello?"

"Is Celia there?" It was Bernice.

Derbier hesitated. He didn't want Bernice to come here and see his house like this. She had never come before. She might not even know where he lived. "Why are you calling now? It's four in the morning."

"What? Oh, the time. Is she asleep?"

"No."

"Is she there?"

"She's out," he said.

"She's out at four a.m.?"

It occurred to Derbier that Bernice hadn't heard his message and, so, wasn't calling from the Savannah house. She must be in a different time zone, he thought. It must be far away. "Where are you?"

"It doesn't matter where I am," she said. "I need to talk to Celia. She needs to call me this morning."

"What about?"

"That's between me and her."

"Well I've got some shit to say to her myself," he said. "You know she threw a party here. My whole house is wrecked."

"You bought a house?"

"Yeah," he lied. "Well—you're going to buy my next one."

"How do you figure that?"

"I'm telling you, your daughter trashed my place. There's water damage. The walls are beat to shit. She burned my bed."

"Where were you?"

"What the fuck did you say?"

"I said, where were you when this party happened?"

"What the fuck does it matter where I was? Where were you?" He could hear people talking in the background. He imagined Bernice in the lobby of a fancy hotel in Italy, talking to him on a golden telephone and standing on a marble floor. He imagined who she was with and all the things they had that he didn't. "Where are you right now?"

"Nowhere you can find," she said. "You've got until the end of the day to have her call me. She'll know the number."

"What do you mean, 'You've got until'? Who are you ordering around?" he said, but there was no reply.

"You and whatever sugar daddy you're sucking off is going to pay for this damage," he said. He wanted to hurt her. He wanted her to feel ashamed for living in comfort while he was here with his feet sticking to the kitchen floor. "You can send him my compliments for all I care. Just have him send me a check when you're done. Or else I'll have my lawyer come get it. Do you understand me?"

After a moment, the phone blared the busy signal in his ear. It might have been a minute since she hung up.

"Goddamnit!" Derbier shouted. He slammed the phone against the wall and satisfied his anger for a split second as its plastic shell broke and heavy metal innards scattered over the floor. He slumped against the wall and wondered what Bernice had meant when she said he had until the morning to get Celia on the phone.

He looked through the split blinds at the squat houses of Sea Wall. In the glow of the few street lamps that hung over the road, he could see the old blue truck that was always parked outside of Darlin's house, so she hadn't left town. He had never spoken to Darlin directly, but he had seen her with the young Black man that lived on the island and sometimes lurked around the marina or the houses, feigning handyman work and smelling like weed.

In his bedroom, Derbier found his nightstand where it had been thrown into the closet. The doors were broken and jammed closed, and Derbier lifted them from their hinges and leaned them against the wall. His father's suits hung like stiff, gray ghosts, and he tried not to breathe while he pulled the nightstand out and set it on the floor. He hated how they smelled, but superstition wouldn't let him throw them out. Bernice had said it was bad luck.

The spare truck key was gone along with the pictures he'd taken of the hippie woman, Whistle, and her tiger. He kicked the dresser over. Then he picked it up and shattered it on the floor. Celia was on Bomb Island. The missing photographs confirmed it.

Why would Celia do this to him? Why would she turn on him for the sake of an old woman she didn't know who lived, like a crazy person, in a shack in the woods?

Behind his father's suits was a tall, heavy gun safe. Derbier put in the combination and swung the door open. His hunting rifles and shotguns were lined up neatly, the blued metal oiled and clean. A handgun in a slim holster sat alongside his neighborhood watch camera, an expensive night vision rig he had bought at a gun show. The lens was over a foot long and the camera itself was covered in dials and buttons that he didn't understand, but he had learned enough through trial and error to see what he wanted. He clipped the pistol onto his belt.

He would have to appear in court in a week, and he knew he would likely spend time in jail. It would make things a lot worse if he were found carrying, but he wouldn't go to the island unarmed. He could only guess how many 9mm pistol shots it would take to bring down a tiger and slipped the leather sling of a deer rifle over his shoulder. He was not the problem, he told himself. He was the solution.

Fourteen years of fatherhood had passed in a flash, and the gap between Celia and himself had grown extreme. He knew he had played his part in the hostility that defined their relationship now, but he felt he had never been given the chance to repair things. Lately he felt that he was at the end of his rope. He had made his run at wealth and a family and failed to keep either, but here, now, was the opportunity he had been waiting for.

He had been wronged. He had been attacked on his own property by his daughter and a homeless child. He had been dragged into this, but he would show Celia now that he was still the capable man he had been when she was small. He would show her that there was no end to what he would do to protect his family. The damage to the house could be paid for and repaired. He would see to that. What was important now was getting Celia back. He knew she was scared of what he would do. That was why she had taken the keys and the photographs.

He would show her that he could be fair, and then they would understand each other. They wouldn't have to hurt each other anymore. They could talk. It made sense to him that all this misfortune would happen at once. This was God telling him, grabbing him by the collar and shouting at him: Be the man I made you to be. Fix this.

Derbier pulled on his heavy leather hunting boots and walked with his rifle to the marina. The place was deserted this early. He retrieved his spare key from an empty can of chaw and eased the boat into the river. It thrilled him to be armed and on a righteous mission. It made the soreness in his throat dwindle and the aches from the jail bed dim and disappear.

He circled Bomb Island, looking for signs of life on the ocean-facing beaches through the scope of the rifle and seeing nothing. When he had scouted the island with the night vision camera, this is where Whistle and the tiger appeared the most. He had never seen the main camp, but assumed it was nearby.

Derbier let the boat drift in light chop and studied the woodline where a horse emerged. While the horizon warmed and grew pink, he trained his crosshairs on the horse's face. Through the eye of the rifle, he could see it was a nervous mare. The horse flicked its ears in the stiff, windward breeze. It looked over its shoulder and then, suddenly, broke and ran into the dunes.

He thumbed the safety off and waited for whatever had spooked the horse. His heart hammered in anticipation of the white tiger. Getting rid of it would be Derbier's way of reestablishing himself in Royals, and there would be nothing Whistle could do about it. He would be a legend, and her time skirting the rules and living a freeloader's fairy tale would be over. With the tiger gone, it would be no trouble to go ashore and take Celia.

His daughter was soft for animals and would not understand, but it didn't matter. What mattered the most was respect and loyalty. In some ways, he knew he had failed as a father, but that was only because Bernice's divorce had upset the natural order. She had removed him from the home and removed Celia's chance at a normal life with him. If he didn't right Celia's path now, there was no telling where she would stray to.

On the beach, he watched the mare flick her tail and stomp in agitation, but no tiger appeared. A small brown horse stepped from the woods, then two more. They followed the mare over the dunes and then galloped, the four of them, down the shore as the day's first light fell hard on the beach.

Derbier squinted and spit his chaw over the side of the boat. He slung the rifle over his shoulder, slid the throttle to three-quarters, and resumed circling the island. He didn't want to wander the interior blindly. He had been ashore on Bomb Island once, many years ago, for a hog hunt and remembered the place as a moss maze. Now he fantasized about jungle warfare and creeping through the ruins of the old plantation with his deer rifle and stalking the snowy tiger through fields of cotton, left to wild for a hundred years.

He saw the flicker of flame and a thread of gray smoke on the Royals-facing side of the island, which was, but for a few bits of sand, hidden behind in oyster-spiked mud and marsh. Even from over a hundred yards, he didn't need the rifle to see that a group of people were sitting around the fire.

With the rifle laid over his captain's chair in the tower of his boat, Derbier watched Whistle where she sat by the boy, Fish. Darlin and the Black man laid against one another, and what had to be Celia was bundled in a blanket on the sand. They were all sleeping except the old woman, who only stared into the fire.

Derbier trained the crosshairs of his rifle scope on the silver dot of Whistle's head. He held his body tight against the gunstock. "Look at you now," he said. "Not so cool."

He swiveled his aim to Darlin and the Black man, who had stolen his daughter out from under him. They were kidnappers, he reasoned. They were criminals living in the woods, and they had his daughter. Without a boat, how would she be able to leave? She was at their mercy. He savored the sweet rush of blood and anger when he thought of the harm Celia might have sustained. He could do anything he wanted to them if they'd touched her. Bernice would have no choice but to thank him when he rescued their daughter, and everything else would fall into place.

Something moved in the edge of his vision. The tiger stepped, like a buck, from the jungle. He watched it lie next to Whistle, but she didn't seem to notice. Even with the boat steady on the glassy flat water, and his aim solid on the tiger where it lay in the sand, he didn't shoot. He was, for just a moment, mesmerized by the vision of Whistle reaching out to rest her hand on the tiger's head.

TWO

The bullet tore through Sugar's abdomen and a thin stream of blood sprayed onto the sand. The tiger huffed and raced, first towards the woods, then back towards the shore. Its claws stretched from its paws and tore deep gouges in the sand, then it crashed into the forest.

"Run!" Whistle screamed to the others. "Go!"

They had all come awake at the rifle shot. Reef pulled Darlin to her feet, Celia leapt over the log she had been sleeping against, and Whistle led Fish by the arm towards the woods, where the others were already running.

There was another boom from the water that was followed immediately by a heavy smacking sound as the bullet buried itself in an oak somewhere in the woods by the camp. Fish looked over his shoulder for the source and saw the profile of a long boat out in the sound and the shape of a man on it. He led Whistle, stumbling, over the sand. He could hear Sugar thrashing in deep cover. He saw him leap into the air.

Reef and Darlin scrambled up a treehouse ladder, and the tiger burst from the woods at a sprint. His head pivoted erratically, looking for what was killing him. He lunged for Reef's foot and tore three rungs from the ladder.

Whistle picked up a chunk of wood and threw it at the tiger. "No!" Fish pleaded with the old woman to climb the treehouse ladder, but she shoved him off and threw a stone at Sugar, who was snarling and lurching up the broken ladder, leaving smears of blood against the light-colored wood. "Go!" she commanded Fish. "Go to Nutzo!"

In the scramble, Celia fell from a rotted ladder on the far side of camp and moaned on the sand, trying to get up. Fish ran to her and they hobbled, then ran for the cover of the woods, but Fish stopped and turned back when they reached the thick of the brush. He could hear Reef bellowing at the tiger. He saw him swinging a plank of wood at the tiger's head. When the board connected with Sugar's skull, it made a heavy thud, but the tiger continued to snarl and climb.

"Run!" Celia wheezed at Fish. Her face was strained and red. The air had been knocked out of her in the fall.

"I can't leave them!"

"We've got to run!" She snatched at his arm, but he pulled away. "I don't know where to go," she cried. "Please!"

Whistle snatched her pistol from a bin by the fire and ran at Sugar, screaming and firing the gun at the long muscled back of the tiger where it clung to the remnants of the treehouse ladder and fought with Reef. One of the shots tore a hole in Sugar's shoulder, and he dropped from the tree to rush the old woman.

For a half-second, it looked to Fish that Sugar was going to lie down at her feet and submit, the way he held his head low to the ground, but the tiger leapt and crushed Whistle to the sand. He buried his face into her neck and tore her throat. Whistle's arms grasped the tiger in an embrace as he savaged her. She never made a sound.

"No! No!" Reef jumped from the treehouse and staggered in the sand. He clubbed the tiger with the plank until it leapt from Whistle and swiped the board from his hands.

"Get away!" Darlin screamed. She hurled books, boots, anything she could find down at the tiger, but it closed on Reef. It leapt and put its paws on his shoulders and knocked him to the ground.

Fish ran for the tiger, but something pulled him back, hard, by the arm and dragged him into the brush. His vision darkened and narrowed, and his head swam. He fell and, still, he was dragged over the sand and into cover. The sharp points of the saw palms jabbed into his body, but he couldn't feel their sting.

"Which way?" Celia shouted over him. "Get up!" She pulled him to his feet.

"What?"

"Where do we go?"

"Nutzo," Fish mumbled.

"What?" Celia grabbed Fish by the hairs on the back of his neck with her unbroken arm. "Where do we go?"

Celia led them through the forest, pulling Fish along by his hand. It was necessary to keep a hold of him as, every few minutes, he tried to pull free and go back to the camp. "We can't help them that way," she said.

"He killed her."

"We don't know that. We need to get to the boat."

Fish stopped walking, and tried to find his bearings. They had been swallowed by the forest. Low oak limbs blocked their path. Palms and scrub trees snatched at their legs. The game trail they were walking was faint. Until this morning, Fish thought he knew every yard of the island, but he was lost. The best he could do was to listen for the waves, so far off, and stumble in the opposite direction. The small cove where they docked the boat was on the island's mainland side.

"Did you see where the shots were coming from?"

"Yes," Fish said. "It was an orange boat."

Celia kept walking in front of him and didn't turn her head.

"I said it was an orange boat."

"I heard you," she said.

"So that would be Derbier."

"I know that. I'm sorry."

"You're sorry? We should have never taken you here."

She turned and tried to slap him, but he blocked her with his arm. "You asked me to come." She swung at him again and connected with his jaw. "I didn't ask you for anything."

"Quit."

Celia sat down and dug at the sand with her hands. "I didn't ask for any of this, Okay?" Tears slid down her cheek in glimmering lines.

In his encyclopedias, there was a picture of an Indian jungle pig that had been hauled into a tree by a tiger and eaten. In the black-and-white image, the pig's hind legs hung skinny and gray beneath the brown bulk of its body. They had been stripped of meat. Fish's guts clenched, then flipped, and he leaned against a tree to empty his stomach.

When he was finished, he wiped his mouth with his arm and turned back to Celia with his eyes bloodshot. He offered his hand to help her to her feet, and she took it. "I'm sorry."

"Let's keep moving."

"We can't go to the boat," he said.

"Why not? We need to get out of here."

"The keys. They're with Whistle."

"So what do we do? Can we, like, hotwire it or something? Is there a spare?"

"I don't know. Nutzo is the only one who would know about those things. That was were Whistle told me we should go."

"You know where he's at?"

"I hope so."

They walked the narrow sand trails for an hour, and Fish looked for the trail that would lead him to the trap clearing. He watched his feet move beneath him like separate animals, shuffling forward and turning down whatever path they liked. From time to time, the two heard the far-off echo of a man's voice, shouting, but they couldn't decide if it was the wind or Reef or Derbier.

At a fork in the path, Fish recognized his own footprints and traced them back to the tiger pit. Celia walked into the clearing, and Fish caught her by the elbow. "Wait," he said. He pointed to the place where the reeds and palm fronds lay in a mat. "That's the trap."

"Where's Nutzo?"

"I don't know." Fish climbed into the branches of the oak that overlooked the pit and found a gallon of water, half-drunk, and a plastic bag filled with pecan shells. There was no way of knowing when or if the old man would return. From the tree's vantage, he could see the ocean-facing beach through a small break in the canopy.

"Well?" Celia said.

"He was here. He's probably nearby." Fish lowered the water to Celia, who drank from it and set it against the tree.

"How do you know?"

Fish scratched his scalp in frustration. "I don't know. I just think he would be nearby."

"Nutzo!" Celia called into the woods. "Nutzo!"

"Be quiet!" Fish said. He listened for Sugar to come ripping through the forest or for Derbier's rifle to strike him dead.

"Nutzo!" Celia yelled. Her voice disappeared without an echo.

He climbed down. He didn't see the cooler of Coke bottle bombs, and he worried that Nutzo had believed, after all, that Whistle would remove Sugar on her own and destroyed the dynamite. Maybe he was, right now, pulling the rubber seals from the top of the bottles and submerging them, one by one, in the southern marsh.

"Stand over there and keep watch," Celia said. She walked back into the brush the way they came.

"Where are you going?"

"To pee. Stay there." She walked into the woods.

"Don't go far."

"Don't tell me how to pee."

Fish paced around the edge of the clearing, looking for the place Nutzo might have stashed the explosives. He dug in the brush and the leaves. He began to despair. He thought of Reef and how strong he was. The tiger hadn't seemed to care when he hit it with the wooden plank. He wondered if the tiger was still there and if it had climbed into the treehouse after Darlin. Sugar had been shot at least twice. He was bleeding, but he wasn't dying. He seemed stronger. Fish felt exposed on the open sand and climbed back into the tree. He thought of Whistle and how she couldn't die. He had been told she couldn't die. He believed.

After a few minutes and no sign of Celia, he began to worry. He shouted her name and waited, but there was nothing. He shouted again, and heard a heavy limb snap. A small brown bird flew from the direction the sound had come. If the tiger knew he was in the tree, he would kill him easily. Fish pressed himself against the bark and made his body still as he could. His blood seemed to rattle his bones, and the sound of his pulse grew deafening. He reminded himself to breathe. He kept his head still and turned his eyes, searching the woods.

There was a hissing sound, and, to his amazement, Fish watched a glass bottle of Coke land, then roll in the sand near the edge of the brush. Its long fuse smoked to the bottle's top, then seemed to go out before a boil of sand and fire appeared where the bottle had been. Fish's ears rang and his vision blurred. It felt as if someone had kicked him from the inside of his stomach. The blast left a hole in the sand. A few flames grew, then died in the damp undergrowth at the edge of the woods. Fish held still to the oak's trunk, deafened but unhurt.

Derbier's large face appeared in the brush. He carried the rifle in front of him, half-raised to his shoulder, ready to shoot. His eyes were large white horse eyes. His clothes were wet with sweat. A purple bruise covered his throat. He stepped into the clearing and snagged his foot in a sticker bush, then ripped it free.

I could kill him, Fish thought. If I had the dynamite, I could do it. Like he tried to do to me. He cursed Nutzo silently for taking the explosives where Derbier could find them, then he imagined Derbier shooting the old man through the back of his wooden mask and taking the dynamite. The fear of Derbier and the gun made his throat shrink to the diameter of a straw, and he crouched in the tree, frozen. He held his breath. He pretended he was already dead.

Derbier grunted when he saw the gallon of water. It had been shielded from the blast by the roots of the oak. He walked across the clearing, just missing the trap, and upended the jug, spilling what he couldn't get into his mouth and wetting his t-shirt further so that it stuck to his gut. He dropped the gallon when he finished, and called out to the woods. "I know you're out there," he said. He pulled at his ear and worked his jaw. "Let's talk."

In the tree, Fish's hands began to lose their strength. He worried that the sweat rolling from his head and chest would give him away, or that his legs would give out.

"Come out now, and I'll take you home," he said. "Celia's safe. Whatever you all had going here is done." Derbier walked from under the tree towards the center of the clearing. He was only a step away from the trap. He fired his gun into the air, and birds fled the branches of trees.

Derbier worked the rifle's bolt action and racked another round into the chamber. He seemed to know where the pit was, the way he stepped near, but never onto, the trap door where the spent rifle casing sat, like a gold coin, on the layer of sand and reeds. If Derbier were satisfied that no one was here, he would leave. If he had Celia, he would take her, and once he returned to the mainland he would become invulnerable to Fish.

When Derbier turned his back and made for the woods in the

direction he had come, Fish leapt from the oak tree and landed in the soft sand. Without looking back, he sprinted for the woods on the far side of the clearing, waiting to hear the crash of Derbier's rifle and feel the heat of his bullet ripping through his back. Instead, there was the sound of snapping limbs and the high screaming of a man who has fallen five feet onto a bed of sharpened stakes.

"Jesusgod!" Derbier moaned in the pit. A rough-cut spearpoint was stuck through the top of his boot. Two more stakes were buried into the thick flesh of his back and buttocks. When he saw Fish looking down at him, he snatched his rifle from where it lay in the sand and fired a shot at the boy, but the rifle kicked from his arms and the scope bloodied his face. "Goddamnit," he cried.

"Where is Celia?" Fish shouted down.

"Help," Derbier said. "They stuck me."

Fish walked around the edge of the trap. He watched Derbier squirm and wince. Blood spread in the sand beneath him. "Fuck you," he said.

Derbier's face purpled. He placed his hands on the sides of his boot and, screaming, tried to pull it free from the bloody point, but the tip of the stake widened quickly and had wedged itself against the leather and rubber of his heavy boots and the bones of his foot. He tried again, and his hands slipped in the blood that bubbled from the top of his boot. "Jesus, have mercy!"

Fish became incensed by the word. It had been Whistle's word. It had been the word she lived by. "Mercy?" Fish saw the short steel shovel where he and Nutzo had left it. He scooped a shovelful of fine, white sand and threw it over Derbier's head.

"What are you doing?"

Fish planted the shovel into the sand at the edge of the pit and pried, so that half of the sand wall fell in on the trap.

"Jesus, what are you doing?"

"I'm digging you a little ramp," Fish said. His eyes brimmed with tears and his mouth twisted into strange and tortured shapes. He broke the sand from the wall of the pit and watched it fall on Derbier like an avalanche.

"Jesus! Help!" Derbier shouted.

Fish ran to the side of the pit nearest Derbier and swung the shovel, and a thin cut opened where the flat of the blade struck the man's cheek. "I said to shut up!"

"Stop," Derbier croaked.

"Why should I?" Fish screamed at him. He sobbed. "Why shouldn't I bury you like a piece of shit?"

"Don't." The blood running from Derbier's scalp and face mixed with the clear snot that hung from his nose and ran over his lips, so that bloody bubbles ballooned and broke when he breathed.

"I'm going to kill you. Me. What do you think about that?"

"My daughter."

"Where is she? What did you do with her?"

"She's fine. She's tied up. Please."

Fish acted as if he hadn't heard. "Where is she?" He dug as he spoke. He laughed, then cried, and threw shovel-load after shovel-load into the pit until he was exhausted and the mess of Derbier's impaling was covered, and then he sat against the base of the oak to watch him.

Derbier bled where he sat. His breaths were ragged. The weight of the sand pressed him against the stakes. He cried out, and Fish stood with the shovel in his hand. Derbier pulled his hand from under the sand and held it in front of his face.

"Put your hand back in the sand," Fish said.

"No," Derbier whimpered.

Fish lifted the shovel. "Put you hand down. I don't want it to get in the way."

"No."

"Fish!" Celia shouted from the forest.

"That's her. She's right there," Derbier said.

"Put your hand down!"

"Fish, help!"

"Go get her! The tiger!"

"Shut up."

Wrath moved under Fish's skin. His arms twisted, and his shoulders shook. He kicked in the sand around Derbier's head until it sat above the ground like a bloody cabbage, and then he pressed the sharp steel point of the shovel to the place where the man's neck met his collarbone. Fish put his foot on the back of the blade, and Derbier began to weep. One kick of his heel, Fish thought, and it would be done.

Celia screamed, and Fish ran to the sound, his legs shaky beneath him. They seemed to move without his say. He found her with her arms tied around a tree and her face against the trunk. She had spat out the handkerchief that Derbier gagged her with and it lay crumpled. The white-stitched fabric looked bright and alien here.

Sugar lay on the ground next to Celia, panting like a dog with blood staining his face and tongue. Fish flew at him with the shovel raised above his head, but the tiger only dashed away, limping as it went. Fish began to chase, but Celia shouted for him to come back.

"Get my hands," she said.

Fish hacked at the knot that held her wrists tight to the tree trunk with the shovel until the cord snapped.

Celia's face was drained of blood. Her arms dropped to the ground. The skin around her wrists bled where the rope rubbed it raw. "Did you do it?" she asked.

"Do what?"

"Did you kill him?"

"No," Fish said, and she collapsed against him. Because she was taller, her tears fell on the shaved skin of his scalp before they rolled to his cheeks. Fish dropped the shovel and wrapped his arms around her. He felt the bones moving in her back. He felt her breath on his neck. The enormous, all-possessing rage in his body pulled back like the spring tide, and he cried on her shoulder until they both sank to the forest floor.

THREE

When Nutzo heard rifle shots, he climbed down from the oak and ran to the treehouse camp. When he moved through the forest, the thick brush seemed to turn sideways and let him pass. The points of the thorns slid over his legs, but did not tear his skin.

He found Reef at the base of his treehouse with his back and face slashed. Darlin had fallen from the tree and broken her leg. He set the bone and splinted the leg, and tied her shirt across the deepest cuts on the back of Reef's neck, where the tiger's claws had torn the banded muscle.

Whistle was dead on her back with her throat laid open and all her blood poured onto the ground. Nutzo carried her body into one of the treehouses and covered her in a sheet, then he lay down next to her. He couldn't sniff her hair. He couldn't look at her face. He could only hold her hand where it lay under the sheet. "I'll be back," he said. Then he loaded Darlin and then Reef into Derbier's orange boat, which was beached at the camp with its engine idling.

"You've got to find Fish," Reef slurred. His skull showed through his hair. "He's hunting him."

"If I do that, you'll die," Nutzo said.

"No I fucking won't."

"Be quiet."

The men at the marina helped him lift Reef and Darlin to the dock. A girl ran to the store to call an ambulance. "What happened to them?" the men asked.

"Boar."

John-Elvis limped from the store and stood at the top of the steel ramp that led to the docks. "Whistle," he shouted. He tried to walk down the ramp, but the tide was out and the dock had lowered, increasing the decline of the ramp until it resembled a straight-plunging slide. The old man couldn't make it down. He clung to the railing and watched with wide eyes.

"Reef," Nutzo said. The younger man didn't open his eyes. "I'll come for you at the hospital."

Darlin stared at him where he lay. She held her fingers beneath his nose.

"Ambulance is coming. Ten minutes," the girl called from the top of the ramp.

"I'll come for you both," Nutzo said, and he kicked the boat away from the dock. The men shouted for him to come back. "There's more hurt out there." Nutzo gunned the large outboard engines.

When he reached the island, the low tide left him no choice but to beach the ugly boat where Derbier had, near the cook fire, and when he did, he found Fish and Celia wandering the camp with

Whistle's gun. He wrapped his arms around Fish and set his hand on Celia's shoulder. He didn't take the pistol. "Thank god," he said.

"Where were you?" Fish asked.

"I had to take Reef and Darlin to Royals."

"They're alive?"

"Yes."

"What about Whistle?"

"She's gone."

"Are you sure?"

Nutzo nodded.

Fish was silent. The sun ricocheted off the dry, white sand and into his eyes. The heat and Whistle made his thoughts crawl, made his legs weak. He felt he should get into the water. He felt he should be asleep or just waking up to find Whistle at her fire, brewing tea. "We need your help," Fish said.

It took over an hour to unearth Derbier. He had pulled himself free from the stakes in his back and buttock, but his foot was still run through. Whenever Nutzo touched the man's foot, Derbier whimpered, then screamed. They dug around the stake, cut it as short as they could, and left it protruding from the top of the boot.

It took all four of them, pulling and kicking and groaning, to get the big man out of the trap, and they collapsed to the ground when he was, at last, on level ground.

"You'll lose that foot," Nutzo said. "Dumb sonuvabitch."

"Take me back then," Derbier said.

"You're too big, I can't carry you."

"Well you've got to. You can't let me die."

"No," Nutzo said. "I'll call the coast guard from Royals. They can find you. You'd do well to make it to the beach. That way." Nutzo pointed towards the ocean-side shore.

"How am I going to do that?"

"Carefully."

"I can help," Celia said. "We can make a thing. We'll drag him on branches. Please."

Nutzo looked at Derbier where he lay on the sand with the stake sticking out of his foot. "A litter," he said. "That's a smart daughter you have, Derbier, but I don't feel like making a litter right now."

"You dug me out."

"Yeah."

"You had my daughter here. How was I to know—" his voice trailed off under Nutzo's flat gaze. "How was I know it would be like that?"

Nutzo stood and walked to the edge of the clearing. He leaned on an oak.

"I'll drag him to the beach," Celia said. "If you'll just help me make the thing."

"No," Nutzo said.

"What do you mean no?"

"I mean no," Nutzo shouted. "No more! Let him crawl." The old man turned and stood over Derbier. He clenched his fist. "Pathetic worm," he growled.

Fish watched Nutzo in silence from the big tree. The old man's shoulders rose and fell with his breath, and his kind wizard's face was bent into a grimace. "I'll help drag him," he said.

"Why?" Nutzo whispered.

"So it can be done."

"What do you mean?" Nutzo asked. He kicked Derbier in the side, and the man yelped. "You can't take a litter to the ocean-side beach. It's too rough. You'd have to drag him a mile back to camp."

"I can do that."

"You could have killed him, and you wouldn't have to."

Fish stared at the ground. "I couldn't."

"Please," Celia said. "Please, Kyle."

"What the fuck did you call me?"

"Please."

"Who told you that name?"

"Let's think about it," Fish said.

"No," Nutzo said. He walked into the brush towards the beach.

Fish searched for two strong poles for the litter. They spread Derbier's massive, bloody shirt flat on the ground and laid the poles on either side of it and rolled them towards the center of the shirt, wrapping them like the spools of a scroll until the shirt was taut between them. The result was a sorry, narrow stretcher, and they labored to help Derbier onto it.

When Fish and Celia both pulled from the same side of the litter, they were able to drag the large man over the sand, but their pace was glacial. The litter stalled over a root in the sand that bit into Derbier's back, and he shouted for them to stop. New blood shined on the dark shirt.

"We need Nutzo," Celia said.

"I know," Fish said.

"He's gone," Derbier whispered. His eyes were squeezed closed.

"Let me try." Fish followed the path that Nutzo took to the beach. He found the old man just a few yards into the brush, sitting on the trunk of a toppled palm and watching the surf. Nutzo's mask glared from the back of his skull. "If we can get him to camp, Celia can drive him back to Royals," Fish said.

"Why didn't you kill him?" Nutzo said. His eyes were puffed to slits. "After what he did."

"Why didn't you?"

Nutzo stared at his hands. He was weaving three pieces of grass into a diamond. "If they took me away, what would happen to you?"

"No one's going to take you away."

"You're dragging him all the way to the camp?"

"Yes," Fish said.

"Over deer trails?"

"Yes."

"You would need a tarp to make the litter."

"I've got it figured."

The old man smiled. He handed Fish the grass star. "Your trap worked."

"Yeah. I didn't know it would be like that."

"What did you think it would be like?"

"I don't know. I thought he'd be dead. He was just really hurt."

"It's not clean," Nutzo said. "None of this was supposed to happen. You used the dynamite. I saw the blast."

"No, it was Derbier."

Nutzo cursed. "It was old. I'm surprised it worked at all. He could have easily blown himself up and saved us the trouble."

"We can still use it on Sugar," Fish said. "He only threw one at me."

"The tiger is dead," Nutzo said.

"What? I just saw him."

"Where?"

"In the woods by the clearing. When I untied Celia."

"And what happened?"

"I ran at him, and he took off. He had a limp."

Nutzo was quiet for a while, he scratched at his messy gray beard. "That was brave," he said. "I'm very proud of you, Fish."

"He was bloody. I don't know why he didn't hurt Celia."

"I don't know either."

The three of them dragged Derbier over the trail without speaking. They stopped often to rest and pass the jug and listen for the tiger. "You won't hear him," Nutzo said between mouthfuls of water.

"He's dead by now," Derbier said. "I shot him through the lungs."

By the time they reached camp, the tides had shifted again, and the orange charter boat was beginning to lift from the sand. Derbier groaned and hissed when the salt water washed into his wounds, then washed out in thin red lines. The sides of the boat's hull were too tall for them to heft him inside, and they were forced to float Derbier to the back ladder, where he could pull himself on board. He sat against the wall of the hull and bled onto the white floor.

"You can get him back?" Fish asked Celia. The sound was deep, but there was a still a risk of running over a hidden sandbar between the island and Royals.

"I think so," she said.

"What will you tell people?"

"I'll tell them what happened. He fell in a trap."

"What about Whistle and the tiger?"

"What do you want me to say?"

"Don't say anything, I guess. You really didn't see Sugar when you were tied up?" He thought maybe, for some reason, she hadn't wanted to say so in front of Derbier and Nutzo.

"No. You really did?"

Fish tried to remember the tiger exactly as it had appeared. The blood had coated its white face and paws. It had seemed tired, but didn't look to be dying or even injured besides the limp. Fish wondered how many gunshots a tiger could withstand.

"I saw him," Fish repeated, but even as he said it, he didn't believe. Why would Sugar kill Whistle and spare Celia and Derbier? He could have gotten to the man easily while he was buried. It didn't make sense.

"Why did you scream?" Fish asked her.

"I thought you were going to kill him."

"Yeah."

"I'm glad you didn't."

"Yeah."

"You can't keep living here if the tiger's alive," she said.

"Will I see you again?"

Celia looked at him seriously. It was a let-me-help-you look. "I don't know," she said. "You've got to be careful."

"I know that," he said.

Fish shoved the boat off the sand and into deeper water and watched Celia motor away with her father. He stared past the boat to the mainland where Reef was, hopefully, alive. Nutzo put a hand on his shoulder.

"What do we do now?" Fish asked.

"We send her off."

FOUR

ish and Nutzo walked to the ocean-facing beach and began collecting driftwood. They stacked warped, white branches and logs into a rectangular mound and layered them with kindling and split, dried pine. When they finished, the pyre stood three feet high. Broken planks and twisted branches lined its sides and sang when the wind caught their edges. The old man and the boy sat on the dunes and stared at what they had made.

"It's pretty," Fish said.

"Yeah," Nutzo said. "She wanted it to be like this."

"She talked to you about it?"

"Yes."

"Will it take long?"

"Some hours."

"You've done this before?"

"Never."

The white woodpile looked like a jagged throne. Fish imagined Whistle burning on top of it. Her long hair melting and twisting around her skull. It seemed awful. When he died, he wanted to be dropped into the ocean, far out at sea. He wanted to ride the great conveyor belt currents that rush past the continents and circle the oceans, day and night. His body would break into tiny pieces and spread over the seafloor. It would drag over dark sands in the polar north, then rise in the tropics. Whistle had told him so.

"The sky is an ocean," she'd said. "And we are the crabs that walk on its bottom."

"Why did she want it like this?" Fish asked Nutzo.

"Why do you think?"

"To rejoin the Earth."

"Sure," Nutzo said. "She wanted that."

"What else?"

"Her mother died in a fire. The same fire that she saved you and your mother from in Atlanta."

"I didn't know that."

"They weren't close," Nutzo said. "The mother was mean as a snake. She never understood Whistle. She would only call her Colleen."

"Colleen." Fish felt the new word in his mouth.

"She baked all her photographs of Whistle in an oven. Burned the place down."

"Why?"

"She saw a photograph of Whistle making love to a woman."

"She hated women?"

"She was hateful," he said. "When she died, Whistle wasn't able to bury her because her husband had fixed it, somehow, so that he was the one to manage the mother's remains. He cremated the body and hid the ashes. Told Whistle he'd taken them someplace safe. She could have them back once she came to her senses. But you've heard about him."

"Did you get them back?"

Nutzo nodded. "I took them out of his house. He had them in a box under the bed. Whistle wanted them—" Nutzo's voice caught in his throat. "I'll put them with her on the fire."

"What should I do?"

"I'll need your help to carry her."

"I can do that."

"Then all we do is say goodbye, for now."

"What'll we do with the ash?"

"The tide will come tonight and take it away. Take them both away."

"Tonight?"

"Yes."

They sat on the dunes and told Whistle stories and cried and held one another until the tide was nearly out and the shore was at its longest. The pyre stood over the vastness of the empty gray beach. The sky turned the color of an iron sheet.

"Let's go get her, then," Nutzo said, and they walked to the ruined camp under a drizzle. The old man climbed into Whistle's treehouse by himself to prepare the body, while Fish brewed black tea.

"I'm going to wrap her in a blanket," Nutzo said from the mouth of the shelter after a few minutes. "Would you like to see her first?"

"Yes," Fish said.

Whistle laid on her back. Nutzo had bandaged her neck and chest with fresh, white gauze, but the air still smelled of blood. She wore a dress Fish had never seen before. Blue with white flowers. Her hands crossed over her chest, holding a wooden box and a small stack of letters, and her hair was down. Nutzo had smoothed it as best he could.

"I wrote down what Reef wanted to tell her," Nutzo said. "There's the paper and pen there."

"Can I braid her hair?"

"Yeah," Nutzo said. "She would like that." He lifted Whistle to his shoulder and her hair fell down her back.

Fish collected the loose strands into a braid like a cable. It scared him to touch her, but he felt her tough, silver hairs between his fingers, the same as they ever were. The frayed gray wires and the smooth white lines. This part of her had always been dead, he thought. It never bothered anyone before.

When he finished, he laid the braid over her shoulder and ran his fingertip over the smooth line of her scar. He kissed the cold forehead. Then he took a piece of paper from Whistle's bookshelf and folded it into her hands. It was a picture of a heron that he had drawn last year—the best he ever drew.

They made a new litter from pole limbs and a sturdy blue tarp, and carried her, carefully, through the narrow trails that led from the camp to the far beach. Whistle's body was swaddled in a white blanket, and swayed in the tarp. In Fish's hands, she seemed to float.

When they reached the dunes, Fish saw the bloodied tiger at the base of the pyre, laying on the hard sand and panting. Nutzo was walking in front, leading the litter, but he didn't see.

"Ahead," Fish said. "At the woodpile."

"What?"

Fish looked again, the tiger was gone. "Sugar," he said.

"It's alright. Don't worry. That's over. Set your end down now," Nutzo said. They were close to the pyre.

Fish laid down his end of the litter and lifted Whistle's body with Nutzo so that it lay on the bed of wood. Shells were set into the corners, and mats of grass cushioned Whistle's back. Nutzo doused the wood with kerosene, then passed Fish a matchbox.

"Wait for just a minute," he said. He laid his hands on Whistle's feet and leaned to kiss her brow. "My love," he said. "You have made my life rich. You have led me to places I could have never known. You have made me braver, because you were brave." Then he stepped back from the pyre.

"Thank you," Fish said to Whistle. He didn't know what else to say. He touched the match to the dry grass, and flames began to weave through the wood beneath Whistle's body. The fire slipped between the limbs and consumed the dry timber, and, in minutes, grew too hot to stand near. The tongues of flame reached, flickered, and died. They made a fireball that ate Whistle whole.

Fish and Nutzo watched the pyre burning and the strong ocean winds tearing down the beach and sweeping the fire to the side like long, living hair.

Horses passed in the woods behind them and ground their jaws in the dark. Ghost crabs peeked from their holes and fled from the light of the fire. The day's last wing of pelicans, their silver bellies barely visible, glided through the smoke that carried Whistle away.

"Reef will pull through," Nutzo said. "Will you go with him to Atlanta?"

"I'd rather stay here," Fish said. His voice was hoarse.

"I don't think it would be the same for you. In Atlanta, there would be more people. You could make friends."

"Will you stay here?"

"For a while. But I'm no tour guide."

"I can do the tours."

"Forever?"

"For now," Fish said. He watched the jewels in the bottom of the fire flare in the breeze. "I know I'll have to leave one day, but I don't want to leave like this. That wasn't her plan. How long did she want to stay?"

"As long as she could."

"I can't leave until Sugar's gone."

"Fish," Nutzo said. "He's gone. I saw the body."

"I know he's alive."

"You've been through a lot. Shock is part of that. It doesn't matter how tough you are."

Fish stood and looked past the fire, into the waves. The sand fell from his legs in a fine powder. He brushed it off, then realized what it was. Not sand, but gray ash. It was Whistle, spread like snow. Fish swiped his foot over the ground and saw the feather-light drift was there as well. He wiped his arms and legs furiously, and the ash smeared black against his skin.

"It's okay," Nutzo said. He wiped his own face and showed Fish his hand, piled with ash. "It won't hurt you."

"It's her?"

"Not really." The old man's tears were black drops that bulled paths through the soot on his face. "This is just part of it."

Behind Whistle's pyre, Fish saw the white tiger crawling in the ocean, trying to hide in the incoming tide that crashed, frothing onto the shore and thinned to nothing before it reached the fire. Sugar must have seen Nutzo's tiger mask and crept around them. He was trying to surprise the men by coming from the water. It was the same move he tried on the horses.

Fish snatched a conch from his feet and rushed to meet the tiger in the water. Behind him, Nutzo called for him to stop, but Fish was already too close. The tiger snarled at him and it sounded like thunder over the ocean. If he ran now, Sugar would cut him down from behind. He dove for the tiger with the conch in his fist, but Sugar disappeared into a wave that crashed over Fish's head and rolled him in the black water.

"Come back," Fish shouted, but the tiger only turned its wounded shoulder to Fish and led him deeper. Fish threw the conch, but lost its arc in the twilight. Then Sugar was gone as well, and the grit-sand bottom slipped from under Fish's feet, and he was twisting under the cold water, trying to keep his head up, but the waves were stacked one on top of another. The moment he pulled his head from under one, the next one fell. He looked for the shore, and saw Whistle's pyre, shrunk to the size of his thumb. The tiger had tricked him, and the current had taken him away.

Nutzo's head burst from the water, and he grabbed Fish around his chest. "Kick your feet," the old man wheezed. "Kick." He held Fish's head above the water and pulled him, horizontally, down the beach, kicking and resting, until they slipped the riptide and waded, coughing and stumbling, back to shore.

Nothing looked right to Fish. The empty beach was unfamiliar. Weird stars shifted overhead. The night was on in full. "I saw him," Fish said, while he and Nutzo lay on the sand. All his strength, it felt like all his bones, had been pulled from his body.

"It's alright," Nutzo said. He lay on his back, breathing hard with his arms spread over the sand and his eyes squeezed shut. "It's okay, now. Don't do that again."

"You don't believe me."

"Help me up," the old man said, and Fish heaved him to his feet. They walked slowly towards the glow of the diminished pyre until, all at once, it was snuffed out by the tide and vanished, while they were still over a hundred yards away. Without the fire's distant light, and the moon behind the clouds, they walked in darkness. The lapping ocean touched Fish's left foot and the pinky of his right hand brushed against Nutzo, and, in this way, he kept straight. He could tell the old man was humming, but the song was swallowed up by the wind.

All that remained of the pyre when they reached it was a few of the large logs they had used as a base, and these were twisted and black, getting shoved around by the rising tide. Constant waves rolled the logs up the beach, then pulled them back. Whistle was gone.

"You said you saw Sugar's body."

"That's right," Nutzo said.

"Will you take me to it?"

"If you want. Would you rather go in the morning?"

"Tonight, if you're able."

Nutzo waved his hand at Fish in the dark. "Let's go then." He led Fish back into the forest and through the labyrinthine game trails that wove beneath the trees, whose branches appeared as a black web over their heads.

Fish recognized the path they were on. It was just outside of camp. He stopped behind Nutzo when the old man lifted his hand to point.

"There," Nutzo said. The tiger's body was stretched in the brush beside the trail. It might have been sleeping, how the head rested between the enormous paws.

Fish set his hand on Sugar's back. It was cold and stiff. Like a white, striped log. He felt the place Derbier's bullet ripped through. A small, clean hole behind Sugar's shoulder. Even with his hand on the wound, he felt eyes on his back. He wondered what he had seen in the woods and in the ocean, if not Sugar. Even while he touched the dead tiger, he anticipated its return. Would it always be like this? A stick broke, and Fish flinched. It was only Nutzo.

"I wanted to do it," Fish said. "Whistle would have liked that better."

"Why do you say that?"

"Derbier was her enemy. She loved Sugar."

"She loved you. She didn't want you to be like Sugar, always killing, or holding grudges. She moved here to get away from all that, all the violence we were caught up in. Finding peace was her plan."

"Well, plans change. Derbier came at us. Sugar—" Fish looked at the blood caked and dried on the tiger's fur. It looked just as it had when he saw Sugar next to Celia in the woods. "If I had killed him sooner, if you had told me about the dynamite sooner, I could have saved her."

Nutzo sighed and sat in the leaves next to the boy and the body of the tiger. He brushed a mosquito from Fish's cheek. "Maybe you could have, but it would have broken her heart."

"She would have gotten over it. She would be alive."

"Maybe," Nutzo said. "Or you might have died."

"I could do it!"

"I know. I know you could do it. But would you have done it if she asked you not to?"

"She couldn't see him for what he was," Fish said. "She loved him too much."

"She believed in powerful forces. She believed this island was a special place where those forces came together. The bomb and the tiger and us in between. She knew he was dangerous."

"Then why would she want him here? What did he ever give her?" He had his fist closed around Sugar's ear.

"She didn't want a pet. She wanted to see something free, and she accepted what came with that. She asked you to accept it too, and me and Reef, and because we loved her, we stayed."

"Selfish," Fish said. "Why didn't she see this coming?"

"She wasn't a prophet. She wasn't invincible. She was just a dreamer. And she loved you."

"If she loved me, why didn't she stay with me?"

"She did more than that," Nutzo said. "She was going to change for you. She was going to leave her island for you."

Fish ran his hands over the long body of the tiger. He tried to move it. He wished that Sugar would appear again, as he had on the beach, with his eyes wide and dangerous. He wished he could fight him now until he died and found Whistle wherever he and Nutzo had sent her body. He would fight Whistle's mother next. He would haunt Derbier. He would blow like a wind through Royals and explode the transformers on their pinewood poles. But the tiger was dead. There was no one left to fight. "What do we do now?"

"We keep living free. We honor her life. We forgive her mistakes."

"How would she even know?" Fish asked.

"You'll know," Nutzo said.

Fish felt hurt and anger like twin omen birds on his shoulders, digging their claws into his back. He didn't know how to live free. When Whistle had been alive, she had defined his freedom in the black ink of her daily chore lists. Between foraging for mushrooms and snatching weeds from the sand around the garden greens, he had faded into the trees and the beaches and forgotten that he was a human boy. He saw himself as the bright yellow figure of an electron in his science textbook, flying at great speed around the nucleus, Whistle. Jonathan and Derbier and the mystery of the mainland pulled at him magnetically, tried to rip him loose and lose him forever, and now he was adrift.

✳

They fetched tools from the camp and buried Sugar that night where he lay in the woods. After they smoothed the sand over the grave, Fish obscured the spot with leaves, hoping he would forget where it was.

He slept that night on the cot in his treehouse, and Nutzo slept beside him in a sleeping bag on the floor. While the old man snored, waking dreams rose like spirits from the sand of the island and wandered from the woods. They climbed the squeaking ladder and nestled next to him in the narrow bed. A bloody tiger, a woman made of ash, and the heavy steel body of the bomb. They crowded around him and whispered in his ear what he should do next.

The tiger told him where Nutzo had hidden the glass bottle bombs. It offered its back for Fish to climb on and fly to where Jonathan slept in his bed, somewhere over the sound, and showed Fish which window to send the bottle crashing through, but Fish told Sugar no.

The ash woman spread herself over the ceiling and drifted into his eyes so that small, black and purple spots bloomed like flowers wherever he looked. She told him where she had gone, how she'd flown with the midnight dolphins and settled in the bellies of the rays. Whistle had been born in the mountains, but the ocean was her inheritance, and she offered it to her son. "Not yet," Fish told her.

The bomb was silent as ever. It lay in miniature in the palm of Fish's hand. In his dream, he swallowed the bomb like a pill and prayed to know what Whistle knew about mercy and radioactive decay. The bomb sat in his stomach, small as a mustard seed, and then transformed itself into a second heart. Fish willed it to explode, but it would not.

"What can you do?" Fish asked the bomb that was a heart. He saw all the things the nuclear heart could bring. He saw Royals blown away and forgotten. He saw the land swallowed up by the sea. He saw the second heart break open to show the glass cylinder inside that should have broken years ago and set the bomb off, and he felt that, if he tried, he could break the glass and tear a hole in the state of Georgia that matched his loss.

The ocean drew back from the weapon and waited to see what he would decide. The birds on the mainland woke in their roosts and took to wing. The dead tiger grinned and slipped away to the trees, and the ash woman settled on Fish's shaved scalp, and he was free to choose whether to wipe the island away and leave this world behind or to stay.

"Nutzo," Fish said. The old man was snoring. "Nutzo!"

"What?"

"Why won't the bomb go off?"

"What?"

"If Whistle's gone, why won't it explode?"

"She must not be gone."

FIVE

A year passed, and Fish lived on Bomb Island with Nutzo. Twice a week, they filled the Atomic Pleasure Cruise with tourists from all corners of the world and took them to swim with the bomb. John-Elvis took to riding back to the island on the glass-bottom boat and staying the night at camp. After weeks of sausage gravy at the cook fire, he told them that he had loved Whistle, and Fish walked him through the deer trails to the place they gave her to the sea.

Derbier disappeared from Royals. His house sat empty, and the frame of his bed rusted in the yard until a new tenant moved in and hauled all the fisherman's broken things outside to be carried away in trucks. Fish heard he had moved his business to Florida, but no one knew about Celia. Most were surprised that Derbier had a daughter.

In the fall, Darlin and Reef had a child, and Fish and Nutzo drove to Atlanta to stay through the winter. They sat up long nights on the thin carpet of Darlin's aunt's basement and whispered old island stories. Long, purple scars covered the back of Reef's neck and stretched down his back. His left hand would no longer close.

"They call me Grizzly Man at work," Reef said.

They were comfortable in the city. Nutzo watched the baby while Reef and Darlin worked, and Fish took a job washing dishes with Reef at the restaurant. He went on dates to Lenox Mall with a girl named Roseanne. He drank beer and bowled with the busboys on the weekends. He learned from Reef and Nutzo where his mother's old apartment had been, and he paid a taxi to take him there.

The burnt duplex had been bulldozed and a library built in its place. Fish sat at the cold wooden tables and piled them with all the things he wanted to know—how to build log cabins, and how water moved beneath the ground. Where the red knot sandpipers spent the winter before they flew to Bomb Island in the summer. He piled books next to his cot in Reef and Darlin's basement and read through the nights when the sounds of the street kept him awake.

He spent whole days riding the metro and staring out the window at the glass towers of Atlanta rising from the forest that surrounded the city, and he remembered that he loved the warm glow of the underpass lights. He wandered the length of Oakland Cemetery, looking for quiet, but the city blared at all hours behind the thick brick walls. Beneath a statue of a horse in a field of war dead, he kissed Roseanne, but he was thinking of Celia. He wrote John-Elvis asking if he had seen her around, but he hadn't.

In the second summer after Whistle died, Fish returned to Bomb Island alone for the touring season. Nutzo had grown attached and couldn't leave Reef and the child. When he wasn't touring, Fish worked for John-Elvis, repairing the splintered dock, stocking the live wells with bait, and doing whatever else the old marina man needed. He built a home for himself in the thick of the forest where he could listen to the waves through the trees while he read.

He studied the ocean. He obsessed over maps of the intercoastal waterway and read the diaries of people who had spent their lives at sea, and when he walked to the dunes to watch the horses browse and play, he stared restlessly at the long face of the continent and the open water. He felt the limits of the shore. He longed to see an animal that he hadn't already drawn a dozen times in his sketchbook, and he bought the green sailboat from John-Elvis to carry him where he wanted to go. All through the summer, he let the boat's tall, white sail fill with wind and take him up and down the green marsh coast.

A woman named Cecilia Martin registered for his Sunday tour, but when the tourists filled the cracked bench seats of the Atomic Pleasure Cruise, Celia wasn't there. He found her at the dock when he returned. She was standing at the base of the steel ramp with a hiking backpack at her feet. Her dark hair was dyed purple to its ends and reached her shoulders. New tattoos of all colors covered both of her arms to the wrist.

"Can you take me to the island?" she asked him. "I've already seen the bomb."

Now Fish was the taller one. He had grown out of the mohawk he'd worn to Celia's party, but he still kept his head buzzed in the summertime. A thin mustache feathered around the mole on his lip, but his stomach had grown long and flat. His wiry arms wrapped Celia in a hug and he felt, for the first time, both of her arms around him.

She said she had come to see the horses, and they spent the next three days and nights stalking the scattered band that remained on the island, all across the beaches and through the forest and in the pastures outside the old plantation grounds. They slept in separate sheets with a bug net tented over them and talked.

To Fish, she seemed to come from a dream, and he worried that Sugar would reappear with her, but the tiger stayed gone. Fish studied Celia's tattoos. He couldn't remember which had been there before. She showed him the three-eyed barking dogs and blind dolphins on her arms. On her leg, lasers streaked from the fingertips of the grasping alien arm and converged to form a poisoned apple. She said she tattooed for a parlor in Savannah.

"I've put one hundred and thirty-six eyeballs onto human bodies in the past two years," Celia said.

"Just eyeballs?"

"It's a cash cow. How is your sun holding up?"

Fish showed her the gray circle on his ankle. He barely thought of it anymore. "It's there. How did you finish the tiger?"

"I didn't," she said. "I figured, if you hadn't gone crazy, we could finish it here."

The inside of Fish's cabin glowed in the light of conch candles, the same shells that had lit his treehouse years ago. A small wooden desk sat against the wall across from a narrow bed and a woodstove that John-Elvis helped him make. Sketches of shorebirds and sea maps covered the walls beside two hanging bait nets. A pair of mud-splattered rubber boots stood by the door.

Celia lay over Fish's cot with her back under a light. The half-finished profile of Sugar glared out at Fish and the room. In some places, the ink seemed to have evaporated from Celia's skin. In others spots, it spread under the skin from its heavy lines to make gray blurs. It was rough work done by an untrained child, but, to Fish, something of the tiger—the imperious way Sugar had held his head—was there too. "Good lines, considering," Celia said.

"I'm surprised you want me to finish it. All the artists you must know."

"It's about more than how good it looks."

The image of the tiger transported Fish to the killings and Celia tied to a tree, screaming, while he pressed Nutzo's shovel into Derbier's neck. He had never visited Sugar's grave. Months had passed since he had last seen the old camp and its mildewed treehouses that had begun to fall, one piece at a time, from their trees.

Fish pulled his wicker-backed chair close to the cot and drew in the tiger's last stripes with a fine-tipped marker. He found the dog-legging line of Sugar's back leg and the small flats of his heavy feet. He held up Whistle's tarnished mirror for Celia's approval.

"Good. What else?"

"What do you mean?" Fish asked.

"It needs something else. Maybe a bird?"

"I don't think so. Maybe a UFO?"

"I have a dozen UFOs. Literally."

Fish put the marker to Celia's back. Just above Sugar's head, where a halo might have rested, he drew the shape of the bomb.

"Alright," Celia said. "Engage Model 5.0."

Fish thumbed the large, red switch on Celia's tattoo gun. It looked like a pistol, the way the metal was blued and thin strips of wood wrapped around the handle. "You made this gun?"

Celia nodded. "We call them 'machines,' not guns. I commissioned it," she said. "But the design is mine."

He touched the needle to her skin and began to trace the marker. He struggled to remember just how he had held his hand, years ago, to lay the ink, but he was timid with the heavy machine. He wiped Celia's back and began again.

"You got this," she said. "Don't rush it."

He tried to see the tiger and not Celia's skin beneath it, but the heat from her back was leaching into his hands. His blood seemed to spin in his brain. "I thought you'd be gone. Maybe with Berny. You didn't seem like you wanted to stay."

"I stayed with her for a little while, and it was fine. You are looking at the proud owner of a goddamn GED. I'll try for art school in the city next year. I met some good people. Good artists. You're out here all by yourself?"

"Sure."

"For how long?"

"I don't know. I'm thinking of sailing away."

"Where?"

"North," he said. "There are barrier islands in the Carolinas where no one has lived for three hundred years. There are horses in Virginia. I could winter in Portland, Maine, and then cross to Iceland. See the aurora."

"In the Atomic Pleasure Cruise?"

Fish laughed. "In a sailboat."

"That's what all this is?" she gestured to the maps on the wall, and Fish nodded.

"Don't you get lonely?"

"I'm a tour guide," Fish said. "I meet new people all the time. I write letters. I'm a good pen pal." He wiped the ink from Celia's back and leaned against her side. He dipped the needle and set stripes into the tiger's tail. "I'm alright."

"You seem alright. She would have been really proud to see you like this. Living out here. Whistle, I mean."

Fish shrugged. He could tell she hadn't wanted to say the name. "I don't think she had much of a plan for the future, and she hated cabins. She said they always find mice."

Celia turned her head to him. "Well?"

"She liked living low-impact, is what I mean." The bomb hung over the tiger's head like a cloud or a thought. Like the head of a hammer falling.

Fish focused on the lines that passed between tiny, red freckles on Celia's back. He filled and repaired the places his hand had jerked or skipped years ago. Celia closed her eyes on the cot, and Fish worked for an hour in silence. He learned the weight of the ink lines as he made them. For his cadence, he took the long, steady breaths that Celia drew. Soon, the tiger stretched across her back, complete. Without wanting to, Fish saw the bloody path of Derbier's bullet through the tiger's side.

"Did Derbier lose his foot?" Fish asked. He wiped Celia's back and spread an ointment she had brought over the new tattoo.

Celia nodded. "He wears a rubber peg."

"Does he still fish?"

"I guess. I haven't fished with him. He's Tampa's problem now. He's married again. I know that."

"Asshole," Fish muttered.

"Who cares what he does, is what I think. He's got a right to try again if he can find someone to try with."

"He shouldn't be with anyone," Fish said. He thought of all the lovers Whistle had in her life and how she wouldn't have any more.

"Well what should he do then?"

"I don't know. Volunteer somewhere, I guess. He could pick up all the broken glass in the parking lots. Scrape the gum off telephone poles. Do something useful with himself."

"I get it," Celia said. "He deserved what he got."

"He deserved more than that," Fish said. The last time he had seen Derbier was in a dream. He had fallen asleep watching a movie on Reef and Darlin's couch and seen Celia's father die in a pit of green snakes. In the dream, Derbier cried out for Fish to save him. He waved his arms in the pit like a drowning man while the snakes struck him. When Fish tried to pull the man out with a limb, Derbier jerked him into the pit with him. The grinding of Fish's teeth had woken him.

"He's old now," Celia said. "He got old quick."

"What happened to zero tolerance?"

"What are you talking about?"

"I'm talking about him breaking your arm," Fish said. "At the party, you said it would happen again. That was why we stopped him."

"I don't think I said that."

"He was out of control."

"Alright."

"He was an animal."

"He didn't break my arm," Celia said.

"What?"

"It was a guy I was dating who slammed it in the door, not Derbier."

"You told me it was your dad."

"Well, I didn't know you then."

Fish sat back in his chair. He stared at the tiger on Celia's back, how its wet, black body stretched between a constellation of red freckles, and he saw, again, the tight red skin of Derbier's neck under the bright steel of the shovel head. "He never hurt you?"

"Not like that," Celia said.

"What about chasing us with a shotgun?"

Celia shrugged. "It's over."

"It's over for you," Fish said. "I'm still here, and Whistle isn't. That's because of Derbier."

"Yeah," Celia said. "I know."

"And he's just out there, free and fishing. I wonder what he tells people when they ask him about his leg. I bet he's got some big story worked out. How he fought a man-eater or something. Bastard." Fish scratched his scalp and said, aloud, what he had been thinking for two years. "If I hadn't kicked him at the party. If I hadn't taken you with me to the island. He would have never come here."

"You don't know that."

She was right, but Fish couldn't stop himself. It didn't seem to matter—the year in Atlanta and the library and his plans for the sailboat. It was like all of that were nothing, and he was Fish the boy again. Angry and misunderstood again. On the island with Celia again. Whistle dead again. It had all been waiting for him. "Whistle had a plan. All she needed was a few more days."

"It wasn't your fault. The tiger killed Whistle."

"How can you say it's not my fault? You know what happened. Whistle let you stay because I brought you here. I brought you here because Derbier was going to hurt you."

"I had him handled. I told you to go. You kicked the shit out of him."

Fish put his head in his hands.

"You made your choices, and Derbier made his," Celia said. "Whistle knew the truth about my arm. I told her after you ran off that night. I saw the stuff on that camera, and I told her about that too."

"What? Why?"

"Because I was worried about you. I was going to tell you, but then everything happened. I was angry, and she helped me. She listened. I could tell she was worried about you too."

Fish thought of his last hours with Whistle on the beach. She had warned him about his anger. Maybe she had the same snake dream he had in Atlanta. Maybe that was why she ignored the omen that could have saved them. Why hadn't she known what was going to happen? Why had her magic stopped a bullet but let Sugar through?

"Did you just tell her?" Fish asked. "Or did you show her the video?" He didn't want Whistle to have seen what Jonathan did to him or to hear the things Fish had told him about the island. He had only told simple things: What they ate. Where they got their food. How they washed. Simple facts that unfolded into the happiest memories Fish knew. He didn't want to think that in their last moments together, while she was shouting for him to run from the tiger, that she was thinking of him in the video, helpless, caught in a trap.

"I told her," Celia said.

"Good," he said. "Not that it matters now."

"It does matter, because—even though that happened to you— you made the right choice. You spared Derbier's life," Celia said. "You don't have to live in exile."

"I'm not in exile."

"What do you call this?"

"Living. Making my own choices. What would you call getting a GED and tattooing eyeballs?"

"Just a regular afternoon." She craned her head to see the tattoo. "Put a bandage on this."

Fish rubbed the tiger with ointment and covered it. Thinking of the video made him as angry and confused as when he was a child.

"Relax," Celia said. Their first night in the woods with the horses, she had taken his hand when he'd left it resting in the sand between their bedrolls. On the third night, she had kissed him while they finished the sketches they'd made in the field. He didn't know what these gestures meant, if they were love or just leftover adrenaline.

He knew her return was as natural as the tide, and that when she moved on tomorrow morning, he would be expected to do the same, and he would. He would leave and come back, leave and go. He never planned to stop moving for long. There was too much to see.

"Well then we agree," he said. "We are where we want to be."

"You could come to Savannah," she said. "I know some people who can put you up. You could finish school. What are you? Seventeen?"

"I don't want that."

"You've got to do something. John-Elvis and the tours won't last forever. Come where you've got friends. Where you're safe. Where there's no mice."

"Celia."

"I just feel like I need to say these things. I want to help you."

Fish's anger fell away. He went to his desk and came back with Whistle's journal. He set the book on the bed and flipped past blocks of notes and doodles of coral reefs, fragments of poetry, and the schedules that she had drawn up specifying just where they should be and when. At the back of the journal were pages of names with addresses and telephone numbers set next to them. The addresses were located in cities all over the world. Boston and London and Morocco. Each name that Fish had received positive contact from, he marked with a star.

"Friends of Whistle?"

"Yes," Fish said. "I'll be visiting them."

"How are you going to get to all of these places?"

"The sailboat."

"You can do that?"

"I think so. With some help and planning. This woman"—he pointed to a name on the list—"has a house in Massachusetts. There's a sailing school there. On the cape."

"When do you leave?"

"Whenever I want," Fish said. "Come with me."

"I can't just leave like that."

"Why not?"

"School. My mom. My friends. The plans I've made for my life. I can't just go."

Fish nodded. "Maybe not."

"Alright," Celia said.

"Do you want to see the boat?"

The green sailboat sat next to the Atomic Pleasure Cruise in the tidal cove. *Deluvia* was written across the stern in faded, golden script. Fish had not named a home port. The wood floors of the deck were sun-damaged and broken in some places, but the hull was sound, and the sailcloth was new. Fish and Celia sat on folding, wooden chairs and swatted mosquitos and scratched at their hair for gnats and drank the wine that Fish brought from the dark cabin of the boat. Far off, the lights of Savannah bled into the thick chain of clouds that wrapped around the sky.

"Why didn't you kill Derbier?" Celia asked. She lifted the mosquito netting over her face to drink, then slid it back down.

"I didn't want to kill him," Fish said. He drank from the wine. "I wanted Whistle back. I didn't know how to make it right. After everything. And Derbier wanted me dead. I didn't know if he would stop. It seemed like I had to kill him. Then you screamed, and I thought Sugar had you. I saw him by your tree."

"I remember."

"When I saw Derbier in the pit later, when Nutzo was going to finish him, I guess I had enough time to choose what to do. If we had killed him, none of this would have been possible," he nodded to the island. "Reef and Darlin's baby—maybe that wouldn't have happened. Killing Derbier would have followed us forever. I can say that now, but, when it mattered, it was you that stopped me."

"What are you going to do with yourself?"

"Whatever I can."

"What about when you stop?"

"Stop what?"

"Living like this. Get a normal life."

"Do you want me to?" He lifted the mosquito netting over his face, then Celia's, and kissed her.

"No," she said. "I guess not."

They stayed that night in the cabin of the sailboat, holding on to one another. When dawn came, they rose and drew water from the stinking island well and shared a drink. They guided the sailboat through the narrow cove and into the open Atlantic, past the skeletal horses on the beach and the shell of the bomb. The warm wind followed them. Far off, the gray backs of dolphins broke over the waves. An osprey crossed their bow, and Fish took it for a sign.

ACKNOWLEDGMENTS

This book was made possible by the time, expertise, and counsel of many writers and readers. Foremost are Tom Franklin, Chris Offutt, and Erin Drew, who served as my thesis committee at the University of Mississippi, where the first drafts of the book were written; my generous and talented MFA fiction cohorts, among them, LaToya Faulk, Tyriek White, Victoria Hulbert, and Chris Morris; Skip Horack, whose notes helped my manuscript turn the corner at the final hour; Matt Bondurant and Seth Tucker, whose Longleaf Writers Conference allowed me to share the project with writers such as Wendy Rawlings, Barrett Warner, and my fellow workshop members, Solange Jazayeri and Ruth Pettey Jones; Denton Loving, who provided his excellent ear and allowed me to edit in the isolation of his apple grove as part of The Orchard Keepers Residency; Silas House and my fellow workshop members at the Looking Glass Rock Writers' Conference; Matthew Thomas Meade and Dan Leach, my constant readers and friends; Ward Bowles, one of the first people to see the book; Brian Adams and Kevin Brewer, who explored Cumberland Island with me; Michelle Pillow, for her savvy; Bailey Pillow, for lending her artistic vision and skill to this project; my family, for their unwavering support; and, lastly, to Kate McMullen, Med Reid, and everyone at Hub City Press for bringing these characters out of my head and into yours.

HUB CITY PRESS is a non-profit independent press in Spartanburg, SC that publishes well-crafted, high-quality works by new and established authors, with an emphasis on the Southern experience. We are committed to high-caliber novels, short stories, poetry, plays, memoir, and works emphasizing regional culture and history. We are particularly interested in books with a strong sense of place.

Hub City Press is an imprint of the non-profit Hub City Writers Project, founded in 1995 to foster a sense of community through the literary arts. Our metaphor of organization purposely looks backward to the nineteenth century when Spartanburg was known as the "hub city," a place where railroads converged and departed.

RECENT FICTION FROM HUB CITY PRESS

Good Women Halle Hill

The Big Game is Every Night Robert Maynor

The Say So Julia Franks

The Great American Everything Scott Gloden

The Crocodile Bride Ashleigh Bell Pedersen

Adobe Garamond Pro Regular
10.8 / 15.3